THE WOMAN WHO WALKED INTO DOORS

Roddy Doyle was born in Dublin in 1958. His first novel, *The Commitments*, was published to great acclaim in 1987 and was made into a very successful film by Alan Parker. *The Snapper* was published in 1990 and has also been made into a film, directed by Stephen Frears. *The Van* was short-listed for the 1991 Booker Prize and made into a film also by Stephen Frears. *Paddy Clarke Ha Ha Ha*, which won the Booker Prize in 1993, was the largest-selling winner in the history of the prize and has been published in nineteen languages. His latest novel is *A Star Called Henry*.

ALSO BY RODDY DOYLE

Novels
The Commitments
The Snapper
The Van
Paddy Clarke Ha Ha Ha
A Star Called Henry

Plays
Brownbread
War

Roddy Doyle

THE WOMAN WHO WALKED INTO DOORS

_V_

VINTAGE

Published by Vintage 1998

First published in Great Britain by
Jonathan Cape 1996

Vintage
The Random House Group Limited
20 Vauxhall Bridge Road, London SW1V 2SA

Random House Australia (Pty) Limited
20 Alfred Street, Milsons Point, Sydney,
New South Wales 2061, Australia

Random House New Zealand Limited
18 Poland Road, Glenfield,
Auckland 10, New Zealand

Random House (Pty) Limited
Isle of Houghton, Corner Boundary Road & Carse O'Gowrie,
Houghton, 2198, South Africa

The Random House Group Limited Reg. No. 954009

www.randomhouse.co.uk/vintage

ISBN 0 0995 0774 9

A CIP catalogue record for this book
is available from the British Library

Papers used by Random House are natural,
recyclable products made from wood grown in sustain-
able forests. The manufacturing processes conform to the
environmental regulations of the country of origin.

Printed and bound in Great Britain by
Bookmarque Ltd, Croydon, Surrey

This book is dedicated to

Jack

At the age of 37—
She realised she'd never ride —
Through Paris —
In a sports car —
With the warm wind in her hair —

Shel Silverstein, *'The Ballad of Lucy Jordan'*

1

I was told by a Guard who came to the door. He wasn't
one I'd seen before, one of the usual ones. He was only
a young fella, skinny and with raw spots all over his
neck.

—Missis Spencer?

He couldn't have been more than twenty. He looked
miserable.

—Missis Spencer?

I knew before he spoke. It clicked inside me when I
opened the door. (For years opening that door scared
the life out of me. I hated it; it terrified me. We had
this screeching bell like an alarm that shook the walls
when anyone rang it. It lifted me off the floor, the
kids started bawling; it was fuckin' dreadful. You were
caught, snared, caught in the act. You looked around
to hide whatever you'd been caught with, things that
Charlo had left in the hall, things he'd robbed and left
there. He changed the bell, after I chewed his ear and
nearly wet myself five or six times a day. Nicola, my
oldest, wouldn't come round the back to get into the
house. She wanted to come through the front door; it
was more grown up. She rang the bell ten times a
minute.

—Forgot me jacket.

—Forgot me money.

—Don't like these jeans on me.

I hit her — she was thirteen, or twelve, much too old
to be smacked — the hundredth time she rang the bell

one Saturday morning. I hit her the way a woman would hit another woman, smack in the face. I was a bit drunk, I have to admit. I regretted it, tried to stop my hand after it had smashed her cheek and come back. She held her hand up to her cheek. It was red where I'd got it. She was stunned; she hadn't noticed me getting more annoyed. They never do at that age — at any age. I was sorry for her but she'd deserved it. I was sorry I was drunk, ashamed, angry; I usually made sure that no one noticed. I couldn't cope; it was only a stupid bell. She said she hated me, slammed the door and ran off. I let her away with it. The new bell was a nice bing-bong one but it made no difference. I still died a bit whenever someone rang it. The Guards looking for Charlo, teachers looking for John Paul, men looking for money. It's hard to hide in a house full of kids, to pretend there's no one there. Bing-bong. Only bad news came through that door; my sister, my daddy, John Paul, Charlo. Bing-bong.) It clicked inside me when I opened the door and saw the Guard. It was his face that told me before I was ready to know it. He wasn't looking for Charlo; it wasn't the usual. He was scared and there was something he had to tell me. I felt sorry for the poor young fella, sent in to do the dirty work. The other wasters were out in the car, too lazy and cute to come in and tell me themselves. I asked him in for a cup of tea. He sat in the kitchen with his hat still on him. He told me all about his family.

2

I swooned the first time I saw Charlo. I actually did. I didn't faint or fall on the floor but my legs went rubbery on me and I giggled. I suddenly knew that I had lungs because they were empty and collapsing.

Charlo Spencer.

There he was, over there, leaning against the wall.

Fiona nudged me.

—There he is.

I saw him and I knew who she meant. It couldn't have been anyone else, after all I'd heard about him, after all I'd expected. He was with a gang but all by himself. His hands in his pockets with the thumbs hooked over the denim and a fag hanging from his mouth. It got me then and it gets me now: cigarettes are sexy — they're worth the stench and the cancer. Black bomber jacket, parallels, loafers — he was wearing what everyone wore back then but the uniform was made specially for him. The other boys looked thick and deformed beside him. Tallish, tough looking and smooth. In a world of his own but he knew we were watching him.

We'd been dancing together in a circle, our jackets and jumpers and bags on the floor in front of us, and I was sweating a bit. And I felt the sweat when I saw Charlo. This wasn't a crush — this wasn't David Cassidy or David Essex over there — it was sex. I wanted to go over there and bite him.

He took the fag from his mouth — I could feel the lip coming part of the way before letting go — and blew a gorgeous jet of smoke up into the light. It pushed the old smoke out of its way and charged into the ceiling.

Then he fitted the fag back onto his lip and the hand went back to his pocket. He was elegant; the word doesn't seem to fit there but that was what he was.

The music. I remember it. Women always do. Sugar Baby Love. By The Rubettes. It was the perfect song, sweet and fast, corny but mean, high-pitched but definitely masculine. Charlo's theme song and he didn't know it. He had nothing to do with it; the D.J. had chosen it, just then and there. And it fitted; it was perfect. Looking back at it now. But I didn't know he was going to look at me. I didn't know he was going to move away from the wall and walk. I didn't know he was going to stand in front of me. I didn't even have time to dream it.

He was coming over. The cigarette went onto the floor; he flicked it away, didn't look where it was going. He was coming straight at me but he wasn't looking. I was shiteing; he was going to walk past me.

—D'you want to dance?

I let him sweat for a bit.

—Yeah.

His timing was perfect. The Rubettes stopped and Frankie Valli started singing My Eyes Adored You. He must have planned it. His arms went through my arms just as Frankie went *My*; his fingers were knitted and on my back by the time Frankie got to *Eyes*. He'd been drinking. I could smell it but it didn't matter. He wasn't drunk. His arms rested on my hips and he brought me round and round.

—But I never laid a hand on you —

My eyes adored you —

I put my head on his shoulder. He had me.

3

I knew nothing for a while, where I was, how come I was on the floor. Then I saw Charlo's feet, then his legs, making a triangle with the floor. He seemed way up over me. Miles up. I had to bend back to see him. Then he came down to meet me. His face, his eyes went all over my face, looking, searching. Looking for marks, looking for blood. He was worried. He turned my head and looked. His face was full of worry and love. He skipped my eyes.

—You fell, he said.

4

I had an older sister, Carmel, and two younger, Denise and Wendy, and three brothers, Roger, Edward and George, all younger — George is still only a teenager, the same age as my Nicola. Then there were my mother and father, Hilda and Roger. The O'Learys of 97, St Francis Avenue. No cats or dogs.

Wendy is dead. She was six years younger than me. She did a bit of babysitting for us; she was great — she'd get up in the morning with the kids and give them their breakfast so we could stay in bed. So *I* could stay in bed. She was lovely, a lovely figure, smashing black hair — like an ad. Nicola and John Paul were mad about her. They never minded when we were going out because that meant that Wendy was going to be staying for the night. Myself and Charlo really went out in those days, not just down to the local pub although we did that as well. We made an effort, went into town to the pictures. We even went back to some of the dances we'd gone to before we were married. For a while. I didn't drink as much then, only when we were out, on special occasions — I can't remember what they were. Wendy was the passenger on her boyfriend's motorbike and he drove it into the wall of a bridge in Wicklow, somewhere near Glendalough. In broad daylight. He lost control of it or something, skidded. He was going too fast, something like that; I don't understand motorbikes or driving. She'd only been going with him for a couple of weeks. Mammy and Daddy didn't know he had a bike. She'd never told them. The Guards came to their door. Eddie came to ours.

It was a happy home. That's the way I remember it. Carmel doesn't remember it like that and Denise won't talk about it at all because, I think, it would mean that she'd have to take a side, mine or Carmel's.

I remember lying in my cot just below the bedroom curtain that was blowing in and out over me; the curtain had flowers on it. The sun was on the wall when the curtain blew into the room. There were noises from downstairs, the radio and my mammy humming and putting things on the table. I was warm. Carmel was asleep in her bed. Denise wasn't born. That's the first thing I can remember. I think it's all the one memory, that it all happened at the same time. I think it's true. I'm not sure but I think there's another part — my father in the coal shed scraping coal off the floor into the bucket, the screech of the shovel on the concrete. If it did happen then it must have been the weekend because the fire was never lit on weekday mornings. I don't trust that bit, because I always loved that noise, something about it, even now — maybe knowing that there was a lovely big fire coming. The cot was white, chipped so that some of the wood underneath showed. There was a picture of a fawn at the end where my head was. I thought it was a dog until years later when my daddy took it down out of the attic for Eddie. When I saw it again — I was eleven — it was a fawn. I checked the chips where the white was missing to see if it was the same cot. It was. When I think of *happy* and *home* together I see the curtain blowing and the sun on the wall and being snug and ready for the day, before I start thinking about it like an adult. I see flowers on the curtains — but there were never flowers on the curtains in our room. I asked my mammy when I was over there last week did we ever have flowery curtains and she said No, they'd never changed them, always stripes.

I told Carmel. The three of us, the three sisters, went for a few drinks — children's allowance day — and I told them, my first memory. She was sneering before I'd finished but it was too late to stop. It was the drink that made me tell it; otherwise, I'd never have told Carmel. She's a hard bitch.

—Lucky you, she said. —D'yeh want to know what my first memory is?

—No, I said.

—I'll tell yeh.

—I don't want to know.

—I listened to yours —

—I don't want to know, I told her. —You can keep it.

I can give her back as good as she gives. It took me years to realise that it didn't matter that she was the oldest; it didn't mean that she always had to be right or that she had to have the last word. She still thinks it matters; that's her problem. I like her, though. I love her. I feel sorry for Denise sometimes, stuck between us. They've been great to me over the years, my two sisters. They won't let me tell them that, but they have; they've been just brilliant. I'd never have done what I did — I'd never have finished it — without them helping me.

My mammy lost two babies between me and Roger; she had two miscarriages. I was 1956 and Roger was 1959. She only told me about them two years ago; I'd never have known. I can remember her smiling, patting my head, picking me up, fixing my dress properly on me, a yellow dress. She never yelled. Would I remember if I'd seen or heard her crying when I was still a baby? It really shocked me. She'd hidden it. She was always so gentle; she'd always had room for me. Carmel says it wasn't like that. She says she knew; she heard Mammy crying in their bedroom. She says that Daddy was never there. Maybe I only remember her dressing me because I dressed my girls, Nicola and then Leanne, the same way. I had a yellow dress for Nicola, and Leanne had it after her; it was still good. (I try not to make my kids wear hand-me-downs.) Maybe that's all I remember, me dressing Nicola, and I'm imagining the rest. But I remember it, the yellow dress. It was too big for me; it must have been an old one of Carmel's.

—I never had a yellow dress, she says.

I shouldn't have asked her.

—I hate yellow, she says.

—Yeah yeah yeah, I say.

I hate it when I say that, Yeah three times like that, especially when I say it to the kids. It's a habit I got from Charlo.

I lost a baby as well.

I liked being cold when I was little because there

was always somewhere in the house that was warm, somewhere to go into; the kitchen or the living room. They were always warm. The cold pushed you into them. We all fitted, in front of the telly or at the table. I had a corner of Daddy's chair that was all my own. He blew his cigarette smoke so it looked like it was coming out my ears. Carmel doesn't remember that either. I don't know how he did it, made the smoke blow in both directions. I never saw him; I had to keep my back to him. Charlo couldn't figure it out either. He wanted to do it with John Paul. He tried it but he just blew the smoke straight into the back of his head.

There was more ice in the winter. Carmel agrees. If we threw water on the path outside the house before we went to bed there was a slide there in the morning. No one complained either. These days they'd sue you. *These days*. I sound like an oul' one. It was more than thirty years ago, though. Another thing I remember that doesn't seem to happen any more is freezing cold feet, cold that would make me cry. I remember being in school early and sitting in my desk and dying for the teacher to come in and turn on the heater because my feet were killing me, they were sore like a car had run over them or something really heavy and cornered had fallen on them. It was the cold. I had socks. I had proper shoes. I had porridge for breakfast. *Pop on the Flahavans*. I smacked my feet up and down and clenched my fists; it was agony. I wasn't the only one. We all complained about it. Mammy said it was growing pains — I think she said that — but it couldn't have been; my toes weren't the only parts of me that were growing but that was where all the pain was, and only in the winter. I've never been able to afford good shoes for my own kids — *good* shoes — and they've never complained

9

about cold feet. Poor Leanne had to go through one whole winter in runners and she never whinged once. She got them drenched one day and I took them off her when she got home from school. I stuffed them with paper and put them up to the fire and hoped to God they'd be properly dry in the morning because I didn't have the money to get her another pair. They were still damp, a bit less than wet, at bedtime so I put them in the oven. I preheated it, then turned it way down and put them in. I sat in the kitchen for an hour and kept taking them out to make sure they didn't melt. It worked. I wanted Charlo to come in and see me, to see how desperate I was. He had money, I knew he did. The smell off his breath told me that. He didn't come home that night, though. I'm almost certain he didn't. (It kills me writing that and reading it — *I could never afford good shoes for my kids*. I don't put all the blame on him, either.) My kids never complained though, and they would have if they'd been really cold. That's one of the good things about living where we live; you're never alone, there's always someone as badly off as you — there are plenty. Now and again it would be nice to see somebody worse off, but I only get that comfort from the telly, the reports from the Third World on the News. The pictures from Sarajevo were very bad but they all seemed to have good warm clothes. I always piled the socks on the kids, two pairs; they liked that. Nicola always liked two different colours so that the inside pair looked like a stripe; it looked very nice. John Paul always made sure that the inside socks were tucked well inside the outside ones, so they couldn't be seen. That's the difference between girls and boys.

There were no surprises at home; there were never any — even at Christmas. We knew what we'd be getting, the present from Santy and our Christmas clothes. I wanted a surprise once — because my best friend, Deirdre, was getting one. I was eight or nine, I think. I let Santy know that I wanted a surprise but I also told him in the letter what I wanted it to be, because Mammy had hinted at what I'd be getting and I didn't want to be wrong. There were no surprises, never any rings on the doorbell or faces in the kitchen window. What was left of Sunday's meat with boiled potatoes on a Monday; shepherd's pie on a Tuesday; I don't remember what there was on Wednesdays and Thursdays; cod on Fridays, with chips from the chipper — we'd have hated the fish without the chips; stew on Saturday. Ice-cream on Sundays; rice on Monday — when I woke up in the morning I knew exactly what was going to happen. I had my bath on Saturdays; I had the water after Carmel, me and Denise in the bath together. Mammy scrubbed, Daddy dried us.

—He didn't.

—He did, Carmel.

—Not me.

—Ah Carmel; he did.

—Uh uh.

—Didn't he, Denise? I say. —He did.

He dried us; he made us disappear inside the towel and pretended he couldn't find us. Half-twelve mass on Sunday, halfway down the aisle on the right side. Daddy wore his blue suit. Mammy ironed his shirt on Saturday night, only his shirt. She did the rest of the clothes during the week, in the afternoon, listening to the radio. Daddy got his Sunday Independent in The Mint after mass, and the ice-cream. In the summer we went to Skerries or Bray after dinner. Bray was the best. I loved the long walk along the seaside and the railings. I didn't

11

like swimming. I didn't mind getting wet but I hated having to get dried. We had picnics on the sand. We never had one of those rugs, the nice checked ones with the woollen frills around the sides; Mammy put all the picnic things on a cardigan or a jacket. I remember it like it's now, biting into sandy bread. It would have been disgusting at home or anywhere else but it didn't matter at the beach. I remember once we had our picnic in the rain.

—We'll stop if it gets heavy.

That was my mammy all over. Daddy went along with her. We were the only people there.

—Can we not go to a shelter?

That was one of the boys, probably Roger, the oldest.

—You heard your mammy.

We got Ninety-Nines or chips before we got on the train home, one or the other, depending on the weather. We all had to have the same, to stop any arguments. A bag of chips between two of us. Daddy made sure that we divided them fairly.

—Your turn. Now yours. That was a massive one he got so you're to get two small ones.

That was the type of thing Charlo loved doing as well, playing with the kids like that. He was really great at it when he was in the mood.

We only ever went on holidays once. I checked, and Mammy says I'm right. We couldn't afford it, she says. We could have gone some years but it would have meant doing without things, and Mammy and Daddy didn't think it was worth it. They began to go more often later, when I was gone and married and most of the others were gone too. They went together to Spain the summer before Daddy died. Courtown was where we went for that holiday. I was thirteen; 1969. I loved it. We had a caravan for a week. We all fitted; the beds came out of nowhere. Mine and Carmel's was on top of the table; it came out of the wall and landed on the table. It was great except for having to go out into the dark to the toilet. The toilet was a big cement block in a corner of the park. The floor was always wet and uneven. They cleaned it every day but the smell always hung on. There was a section for women and a section for men. The boys said that the man's section was woeful. You washed there as well in the morning. There were four sinks in a row. You had to queue up. It was always cold in there. There were no windows, just a bulb hanging from a thick, crooked wire. I loved watching the women washing themselves, the way they could concentrate and talk. I never saw Mammy doing it. She always went in after us, after we'd all been fed and were gone. She wouldn't let us hang around the caravan.

—Go out now and get some of God's fresh air.

That was what she always called the other side of the door, God's fresh air. She still does. She isn't religious or anything — big into religion, as Nicola would say. Daddy never said it. She must have picked it up before she met him. There was an emergency toilet in the caravan but Daddy said he'd kill us if any of us tried to use it. It was only a bucket with a fancy lid on it in a cupboard all of its own. Roger was determined that he was going to piddle into it before the end of the week. He didn't say anything; we just knew. He nearly made it. He had the lid up and his willy out when Daddy caught him. We didn't warn Roger. Daddy dragged him over to the toilets in the dark, and the ground was wet and muddy. Swing boats, bingo and chips. I remember a hill above the harbour and long grass and walking through it. I made a friend called Frieda. She was in the caravan three down from us. Her mammy was real nice; young and lovely looking. She lay on the beach all day and let Frieda do what she wanted and gave her far more money than I ever had. Frieda was an only child. Her daddy wasn't there. She said he worked in South America. I believed her then but I know better now. She lent me her blouse but took it back when I got chocolate on it. We met these two boys from Belfast. I can't remember my one's name; I got the second best. The other one was called Liam. He was sixteen and tall and I thought was he gorgeous. I couldn't understand a lot of what he said because of his accent but that made him even nicer. He was mysterious; God love me. Frieda told me later that she'd felt his thing leaning against her when they were kissing, behind the Crock O' Gold; it was pressing into her. I didn't ask any questions. I only liked my fella because he was Liam's friend. We found out later, after I'd let him put his hand on my breast — on top of my jumper — that they weren't really friends at all. They'd only met just before we met them. They had a fight two days after; my fella beat Liam. It was the first time I'd let anyone feel me. They were real breasts — only boys said *tits*. I had them before I left primary school. I didn't like him touching me but I felt great after it. I thought I'd grown up a bit; I'd got something out of the way. I liked kissing. He hadn't a clue; he just kept pressing his lips into my face. I had to get my tongue into his mouth and go round his teeth and then he followed me. He gasped; I remember it. The trick was stopping before your mouth got too sore, stopping and starting, giving your mouth a rest. Frieda got two love-bites. I didn't get any. My fella

14

wouldn't have known how to give me one. Much more importantly, my mammy would have murdered me.

Carmel admits it: she loved Courtown. She was old enough to go to the dances. I remember her climbing into bed.

—What was it like?

—Brilliant.

—What was the music like?

—Brilliant.

—Any fellas?

—Mind your own business.

Everyone could hear everything in the caravan.

—Go to sleep over there.

Denise has her own caravan now. They have a site near Courtown. They even go there in the winter. I'd love that, somewhere to go. She's never offered; I've never asked. It's not Denise; it's her husband, Harry. He's a bit of a creep. Even Denise thinks that; it all comes out when we're out together.

—Show us your diddies! Paula! Paula!

That was Roger and his pals behind the hedge; probably not Roger himself because he knew I could kill him if I wanted to.

—Show us your diddies!

I kept walking. I made sure I didn't look anywhere near the hedge.

I had my breasts in primary school, in sixth class. Only two of us in the class had them, me and Fiona. We hung around together for months, leaving everyone else out, just because of that — we had breasts. I was dead proud of them after I'd got over my mammy looking at me. It was after my bath on Saturday night; I was standing on the towel, shaking, pretending I was cold. Mammy was rinsing Denise's hair. I started to

15

dry myself. I never rubbed the towel all over me or up and down my back; I hated that. I did one arm first, then the other, then a leg, all the way down to the foot, then the other leg. Each bit had to be dry before I went on to another bit. I never rushed. I saw Mammy looking at me, at my chest. Then at me, my face. I couldn't understand her expression. I thought she was going to lose her temper. She looked away when she saw me looking back at her. Then the part that killed me: she was blushing. She was panicking, it seemed like, the way she dried Denise's hair; she made Denise cry. Because of me. She didn't look at me again.

—Stop fussing, she said to Denise. —You're alright.

She left us in the bathroom.

—She's a bitch for doing that, said Denise. —Isn't she?

—Yeah, I said. —She didn't mean it.

—She did.

—She didn't.

—It still hurt.

I'll never forget it, the look on my mammy's face. It left me feeling like I'd done something terrible to her; I'd hurt her badly and I didn't know how, just that I'd done it.

It was better a few days later.

—Now, she said. —We're going into town, the two of us.

Just the two of us, no sisters, no brothers; I loved it. She didn't tell me why but it didn't matter. I knew from her mood that it wasn't the dentist or doctor or anything bad. I remember one thing that happened on the way into town. I was looking out the bus window at a woman slapping her little young lad. I turned to show the woman to Mammy and it was raining on the other side of the road. I looked back and it was still dry on the woman's side. She'd stopped hitting the child. I didn't understand it then. I thought it was some sort of a miracle or sign; it started to worry me. Then Mammy told me that it was only a sun shower. I can still make myself feel the way I felt when I saw it; it's like missing a last step in the dark and walking into nothing.

We went to Clery's and she bought me two bras. Then she took me into a restaurant and she got me a jam doughnut and a Fanta. She told me not to squirt the bits of doughnut from my mouth into the Fanta because only kids did that and I wasn't a kid any more.

—And you've a bra to prove it, she said; she whispered it, leaned into me, the first time she ever did anything like that. She nudged me. She laughed nicely at me blushing, then I laughed. She looked at me as I shoved the last lump of the doughnut into my mouth.

—The first time ever, she said. —No jam on your clothes. It's all happening.

She was grand when my period came; she explained it all before it happened. The facts of life, they were called in those days. *Those days*; Jesus. She kept me home from school and gave me all the facts. We sat in the kitchen drinking tea. Why I'd bleed, what to do, how long it would last, the pain if there was any. She told me not to worry about any mess, there was nothing that couldn't be cleaned.

—Be ready, she said. —That's our motto.

She gave me a note for school on Monday that said I'd been too sick to go back on Friday after dinner. But I told my friends what had really happened. I was walking a new way now. The Facts of Life. We used to giggle about them; we tried to find them in our dictionaries. We knew it was about things going into holes,

17

and babies and blood. But we never mentioned the blood. We concentrated on the things and the holes. We couldn't imagine it, not really. I still can't sometimes, four children and more than twenty years of sex later. We giggled and laughed and we were scared. Now, in the school yard, I was the first person to have really heard them, the Facts of Life. I'd got there first. The first time I'd ever won anything. It was one of the best things ever to happen to me. The girls standing around me, pretending they knew all about it but some of them looking at me with their mouths open. I said the word Penis like I'd said Desk or Road. Erect. Menstruation. Vagina. Tampon. Headache. Great words; I frightened the shite out of them.

It's one of the only bad things I can remember from my childhood, that expression on my mammy's face in the bathroom, like I'd done something absolutely dreadful, terrible to her. I understand it now though, perfectly. It was just bad timing, that was all; she hadn't wanted me to see that look, I'm sure of that — I'd just been too quick for her. She'd been robbed — that was what she'd thought when she saw my breasts starting; her little girl had been taken from her. That was exactly how I felt when it happened with Nicola, before I copped on and made sure that I kept it to myself. I had a good cry by myself; it was really, really upsetting, thinking of so much of Nicola's life being over, but at the same time I knew that I was just being an eejit. I brought Nicola into town too. Not for a bra, though; the blood came before the body in her case. We went to an over-15s film; I wanted her to feel grown up. Dirty Dancing. I chose it because I thought it would have some nice sex in it; the camera going down the bodies — from the side, no hair — maybe the woman on top for a bit, no grunting; love. She loved it, and so did I. I bought her the tape with all the songs from the film on it. She'd seen it all before, of course, on telly and in videos but this was different, me and her sitting in the dark watching it on the big screen. I nudged her every time Patrick Swayze came on and, after a while, she started nudging me back.

We were never that relaxed again, not since.

5

Gerard was the Guard's name.

—Gerard, Missis Spencer, he told me when I asked him.

—I'm Paula, I said.

—Yes, he said. —They told me.

—Well, they were right, I said.

He was confused, probably wondering if I was joking or not, probably thinking that it wasn't right for me to be joking at a time like this. He ate his biscuit the way a kid does, quickly so that he'd be offered another one. He was slower with the second one.

—Where're you from, Gerard? I asked him.

—Dublin, he said.

—What part?

—Churchtown, he said.

—I don't know there, I said.

—It's nice, he said.

—Nicer than here I'd say, Gerard, is it?

—It's alright, he said.

—D'you live with your parents?

19

—Yes.

—Rent-free.

—No, he said. —I give her two hundred and thirty a month.

I nodded.

He'd forgotten he was a Guard. He'd forgotten to take his cap off. He told me all about his family. His father sold fish to the French; his mammy didn't do much. His sister was in college becoming a vet.

—She's a bit of a genius, he said.

His twin brother was in Trinity becoming something else.

—You didn't go to college yourself, Gerard?

—No, he said.

He blushed.

—It's not for everybody, I said.

6

—He's a ride, isn't he?

I remember it — that's the first thing I ever heard about Charlo Spencer, before I ever saw him. We called every fella that wasn't ugly a ride. A man or a boy had to be in a really bad way, deformed or something, if he didn't get called a ride by us. Even some of our fathers were rides. It was okay for friends to call other friends' fathers rides — if they were good-looking enough. No one ever called my father a ride. It think it was Deirdre said that Charlo was a ride and all the others agreed with her. Deirdre could stare back at fellas in a way that none of the rest of us could manage. It was 1973, coming up to Christmas. I know that because I was working in H. Williams and I'd spent all that day stacking tins of biscuits into huge piles at the end of three of the aisles. I was knackered after it; I remember. I'd tried to open one of the tins; I pulled away some of the Sellotape that kept the lid on but the tape kept coming and coming, there was miles of it. And there was a customer looking at me, a woman. I can remember her. She had glasses that were a bit crooked on her head and her coat was nice; ordinary, black but it looked expensive and warm. I put the tape back on. I could feel my skin burning. I did it slowly so that it looked like something I was supposed to be doing. (It's years since I blushed.) I remember all these things together. The biscuits, the tape, Charlo Spencer is a ride — they all happened on the same day. I know. It was cold too. We were outside The Mint. The type of cold that made you want to go to the toilet, to keep your feet moving and your hands up your sleeves. I think that's why I remember the woman's coat. I was freezing. There wasn't room in any of our houses for all of us. And parents were different then, I think. My parents wouldn't have let us all into the house even if there had been space, if I'd been the only girl and I'd had a room to myself.

He *was* a ride. It was the best way to describe him, from the first time I heard of him to the last time I saw him. He wasn't gorgeous. There was never anything gorgeous about him. When we made love the first time in the field when we were drunk, especially me, and I didn't really know what was happening, only his weight and wanting to get sick; I felt terrible after it, scared and soggy, guilty and sore. It would have helped if he'd been gorgeous, like Robert Redford or Lee Majors. They'd

21

have picked me up and carried me home; they wouldn't have fucked me in a field in the first place, not one of the fields where I came from that weren't really fields at all, just bits left over after the building was finished. Charlo stood up.

—Fuckin' cold.

He wiped his prick on the inside of his bomber jacket, I swear to God he did. I didn't really know what he was doing until the day after when I was calm and thinking about it and making it nice. Gorgeous men didn't do that kind of thing. The grass had been wet. I could smell some sort of animal dirt. Robert Redford would have brought a picnic rug.

He was a ride, he was eighteen, he had brown eyes, he used to be a skinhead, he'd been up in court three times and in St Pat's once. I found out these things that night outside The Mint. He'd a scar where he'd been stabbed —

—On his belly.

—No, his arm.

—It's his belly, said Fiona.

—How do *you* know? said Deirdre.

—Well, if you must know, said Fee, —he's in the same team as my cousin and he seen it. In the shower.

We loved that.

—The shower!

I'd never even seen a shower back then. A shower was like a water bed or a jacuzzi now — there was something rich and filthy about it.

—Imagine tha', girls.

—Soap, soap, soap!

—And a face-cloth.

Deirdre started washing herself, under her arms — she looked around — then between her legs.

—Jesus, look at her!

—Next time, Fee, said Tina, —ask your cousin how long his mickey is.

—Jee-sus!

So I had my identikit of him before I ever saw him; a brown-eyed ride with scars and a record and his mickey thrown over his shoulder. That was how I saw him and that was exactly what I got.

7

The doctor never looked at me. He studied parts of me but he never saw all of me. He never looked at my eyes. Drink, he said to himself. I could see his nose moving, taking in the smell, deciding.

8

The house was empty. Nicola was at work. (John Paul was gone.) Leanne was at school. Jack was next door playing with their young one. She's three years older than him but she loves bossing him around and he loves it too. I had the place to myself. Gerard the Garda was gone. A nice poor young fella.

I wasn't surprised. I'd always half-expected it. Charlo was dead.

He'd been out of the house for more than a year. I'd thrown him out. Out the door. But we'd never done anything about it, got properly separated. I never got a barring order, didn't need one. He was still my husband. That was why Gerard had called. I was still Mrs Spencer.

I made another cup of tea — because that's what you do. I didn't go for the vodka. I decided not to. I put an extra spoon of sugar into my tea.

Charlo was dead.

I picked up the crumbs that Gerard had left behind and put them into my mouth. I don't eat biscuits much. I usually don't have the money for them. I always feel a bit queasy after them.

I could taste the extra sugar.

I still loved him. I'd loved him before I even met him and I never stopped. The minute I saw him, before I saw his face properly, I knew what being in love was. It was dreadful. I was already jealous, already expecting him to leave me, nearly wanting him to be a bastard; I hadn't even heard his voice yet. I loved him when I was throwing him out. I loved him when Gerard rang the bell. I love him now.

Then the shock.

My stomach fell under the table. My ankles ached; my heart charged. All of a sudden. Gerard had told me that Charlo was dead but he hadn't said how. I'd never asked him. I didn't know how he'd died.

I couldn't pick up the cup. I didn't want it. The table was holding me. I had to stand up. I had to know. I wanted people in the house. I wanted noise. I had to find out. It was vital. He wasn't dead yet. I had to know. No tears yet. No tears. He wasn't dead. Anything could have happened. My mouth opened; a scratch came out. I had to do something. I had to find out. I didn't know how. I had to do something. I had to move.

9

I left school after my Group. I ran out of the place; I fuckin' hated it. I stuck it for three years, longer than any of my own kids have done, so far. But I hated it, every minute of it. I loved the primary school. Probably because we had only the one teacher and she was lovely. I can't remember her name, but she was lovely. We all wanted to be teachers when we grew up. It was just girls, fifty-four of us. The noise in the room when the teacher wasn't there, fifty-four screaming young ones. I was good in school, especially at stories. She always got me to read mine out to the class, before she'd even read it herself. I loved that.

—Ah Miss —

—Ah come on.

—I don't want to.

—Ah come on.

She knew I was dying to get up and go to the front of the class but she went along with it.

—Do we want to hear Paula's story, girls?

—Yesss!

Fifty-three voices.

I don't remember any of the stories. What were they about? There's nothing there in my head, nothing. But I remember the applause after and the smiles. I was good in school; she made us think that we were good.

I was only in the tech half an hour when I realised that I wasn't good at all. September, 1969 — after Courtown. We were all kept out in the yard when the older classes were let in. The headmaster stood on the steps and told us to shut up. He didn't tell us who he was; I just guessed that he was the headmaster. He read out all the class lists.

—Class 1.1. As follows. One last time. Shut up.

I was in 1.6, the second lowest.

—O'Leary, Paula.

There were only twenty more left in the yard. I think it started raining. I went past him through the door.

—You'll have the proper socks for Monday, Miss O'Leary, won't you?

—Yeah.

—Yes is the word we use here, Miss O'Leary.

—Yes.

—We also say Sir. Off you go. Down that way. The open door.

Mister O'Driscoll. I remember all the teachers' names. There wasn't one of them that wasn't an out-and-out cunt. The men and women, they were all the same, cunts. Cunts. I hated them. The night before my first day Carmel told me all about them. I didn't really want to hear; she was ruining it.

—He's a creep. He never looks at your face and there's a smell off him.

But she was right. Everything she said was true.

—My name is Mister Waters. W.A.T.E.R.S.

—A dope, said Carmel. —He thinks he's so smart. There's sweat stains under his arms when he's writing on the blackboard. Right through his jacket. He'll spell his name and say something smart about it, wait and see.

—W.A.T.E.R.S. You *are* 1.6 but you should be able to remember that one.

All the different teachers, I hated it. It was much better with just one. I never got used to it. Just one stupid cunt after another stupid cunt all day long. In a smelly room that was either too hot or too cold. I was put beside Derek O'Leary because our names were the same and he walked into the room just before me. He farted all day. Lifted his arse for noise, the dirty bastard. Buck teeth. A smell of sardines out of his mouth. He kept trying to feel me till I punched him in the face and told him to fuck off. I was made to stand up for making noise.

—Well, Paula; it's not very pleasant, is it?

After standing for half an hour.

—No, Miss.

—Sit down.

—Thanks, Miss.

Derek O'Leary gawked over at me and opened his stupid mouth.

—There's a smell o' periods off yeh.

—There's a smell o' shite off you.

—Periods.

—Shite.

—Periods.

—Shite.

For three years.

—Good God, what did they teach you in that primary school?

We were the dopes, the thicks. There was only one class after us, 1.7. They were nearly retarded. You could tell. We were put with them for Domestic Science. You could tell by the way they held their mixing bowls, something not quite right. Two of them were cross-eyed; three of them had stammers. Two of them got pregnant in second year. It was a big thing in those days. They sat beside each other; it was weird. They left school on the same day; they were called out of the class. We were making Christmas cakes. I think. Putting the almond paste on them. They never came back. We said that it was the same fella that made the two of them pregnant. We even pointed him out, a big mallet-head that worked in the butchers. We made him the father. We made him the fathers. He didn't have a name. The butcher, Mister McQuaid — he's still there — never called him anything. He carried the carcasses in and out of the fridge but he never cut anything. Mister McQuaid probably wouldn't let him; it would have been bad for business. The girls were called Sandra Collins and Bernadette Ryan. They never came back. Leanne, my second youngest, started secondary this year. She's in a class called Carolin, after an old Irish harp player. All the classes are named after Irish musicians. We were just 1.6. We got the worst room and the worst teachers, the dopes. They were thicker than us.

It was a fright, finding out that I was stupid. Before I even got in the door. He read out the names, through the Fs and the Gs, up towards the Os, and first five times he went past me and the yard got emptier and emptier. And I wanted to cry. I had all my books. They were all in my bag; it weighed a ton. My uniform, except the socks. Bottle green; I loved it. And it started to rain. All my friends except Fiona had gone through the door into the school. And I didn't like Fiona as much as the others. She was full of herself.

—1.6. Brady, Harold. Brady, Frances. Brannigan, Martin.

It was mostly boys.

—They're all horrible, said Fiona. —Look it.

I was too busy listening, going through the alphabet with the headmaster.

—O'Leary.

I picked up my bag.

—Derek.

I let go of the handle.

—O'Leary, Paula.

The corridor went on forever. I was following Derek O'Leary. He kept looking back. I wanted to go home. I wanted my mammy. I walked in the door. My arm was sore from carrying the bag. A woman teacher pointed at one of the desks that was still empty.

—There.

Derek O'Leary was sitting down by the time I got there. He wouldn't move.

—Move over, you, I said.

He wouldn't.

—Hey, said the teacher.

He slid into the wall and I sat down. Miss Harrison was the teacher. She sat up at the front and clicked her fingers when anyone talked until no one else came through the door. Then, she got up and shut the door.

—Right.

She went to the blackboard.

—Take this down, all of you. No talking.

She was young. That was a good sign, I thought. She wore nice clothes. She was tall. Her hair was up in a shiny bun, like something plastic and black. She wrote Monday on the top of the board and the timetable under it.

—Okay; get that down, all of you.

—Are you Miss Harrison?

—No talking.

She read her newspaper.

—Right.

She rubbed out what was on the board and wrote Tuesday on the top.

—Okay.

—What's M.W.?

—No talking; metalwork.

She didn't look at us. She didn't ask our names. She didn't ask us if we'd had nice holidays or if we were nervous. She was just horrible. I felt Derek O'Leary's hand on my leg. I got away from him. I heard him sucking his snot back into his stupid head. Then I felt his fingers again, taking the material of my skirt. I sat sideways to get my legs away from him. I wouldn't look at him; he was disgusting. Miss Harrison was doing Wednesday but I hadn't been able to get Tuesday down because of Derek O'Leary. He grabbed me again, right up my leg this time because I was turned away from him. It frightened me this time; he wanted to hurt me. I punched him right in the face.

—Fuck off, you, righ'.

He screamed and held his face like it was falling off him.

—What's going on over there? Stand up, the pair of you.

—It was her.

—Shut up.

She came over to our desk. She stared at us, at him and especially at me. I looked back at her. She went back to the desk and picked up the roll book. She looked at me again.

—Carmel O'Leary's sister, she said. —Yes?

—Yes, Miss.

—Another one.

She let Derek O'Leary sit down and she made me stand up for the rest of the class. Carmel had been right about her.

—She has an ice-pop stick stuck up her hole.

She was a stuck-up cow. She put on this face when she walked into the room as if there was a bad smell coming up off us.

—You. Get the windowpole.

She sprayed her perfume around the room one wet day when the coats were on the hooks and the air was warm and soggy. She never corrected our homework; she made us leave our copies open on the right page but she never really looked at them. The only time she ever treated us like real people was the day she came in with her new engagement ring.

—It's gorgeous, Miss.

—How many stones?

—Count them yourself, yeh thick.

We stood around her desk at the front, just the girls, and she smiled and smiled.

—Back to your seats now, girls.

We wanted it to last.

—Is your husband nice, Miss?

—She hasn't married him yet, yeh thick.

—Shut up, you.

—Sit down now, come on; all of you.

That was in the middle of third year, two and a half years after she'd made me stand up. She was back to her normal cuntishness the next day. She had us for maths. I hadn't a clue. It didn't make sense and she didn't care. History, geography, English, Irish — I got worse and worse at all of them. I don't think I learnt one new thing after I went to that school. I wasn't too bad at Domestic Science. She wore a hat in the class, Miss Travers, because she was cold. She was as mad as shite. We spent the whole afternoon cleaning the kitchen, cleaning up the mess left by the older classes. She could never time her classes properly; we'd be just

31

dropping our beaten eggs into the flour when the bell would go.

—Is that the first or the second, girls?

—The second.

—Oh Lord God, time flies when you're enjoying yourself.

She was the best of them. She was wired to the moon but she was harmless. At least she tried to remember our names. She usually got them wrong. She called me Michael once. There were no boys in the class and, I'm not boasting, I never looked like a boy. A mad oul' bitch. She's dead now, Carmel told me. She fell off a mountain in Wales on her holidays. The best thing I remember about that class is Dympna McQuaid, during the Group Cert exam. She had to make a salad, and she did it, finished it perfectly; Travers was sitting on her stool in a corner and she saw that Dympna had managed to get the hard-boiled egg out of its shell and had cut the lettuce without getting blood all over the table — you should have seen the head on Dympna — and she smiled at Dympna and gave her a little sound-less burst of applause — and Dympna went over to the oven, turned on the grill and put the salad in under it before the inspector could get over there and stop her. I'd never smelt burning lettuce before.

Mister Dillon for history and geography. He'd a big drip of snot hanging off the end of his nose all through the winter. You could see the classroom lights in it if he was near enough to you. And he liked getting near enough to us. He'd make us move over and sit beside us and squash in and pretend it was playing; wasn't it great fun, him and some of the boys the only ones laughing, the dirty cunt. Now and again he got us to open our books and we'd read a bit of history. He was filling in our Christmas reports; we were colouring in a picture of someone famous from the French Revolution. I remember the page; 157.

—Pink for the face, remember, boys and girls. There were no darkies among the leaders of the Revolution.

He held his fountain pen over the first report sheet.

—Now.

He wanted us to look.

—A good comment for a kiss. Any offers?

My guts still curl up when I think about it.

Someone pointed at Derek O'Leary.

—He'll give you one, Sir.

—I will in me — I will not!

—That's not what you said last night.

—Enough!

Mister Dillon was in charge again. He's still there. I saw him getting into his car about two years ago. I couldn't see the drip on his nose but he was still wearing the same jacket.

Mister Waters for English. He'd flick through the book.

—What's the point? What's the point? You don't care about poetry, do you; any of you?

—No, Sir.

The prick; I was good at English until he came along with his Brylcream head. He never let us forget that we were dense, that we were a waste of his time. Another ladies' man; he put his hand on my shoulder once and he kept it there and kept it there while he bent over and changed Their to There.

—Tut tut.

He must have felt my heart thudding; he must have.

—Any more Theirs where there should be Theres; mmm?

He pressed his thumb into me. He dragged it over my bra-strap.

—Or Theres where there should be Theirs.

There was nothing exciting about it, a grown-up man feeling me, feeling me while he was correcting my mistakes. The thumb said that he could hurt me, that was all. And I knew the difference between There and Their; I knew it long before I went anywhere near that fuckin' school.

The ones that weren't perverts were either thick or bored or women. That was the only good thing about the women teachers; they didn't mess around with you. They hit us sometimes but it was ordinary hitting. We had Miss Dempsey for English in third year. After two years of no poetry, now we did nothing else. She got annoyed when we didn't like it; she'd wallop us with her book. She couldn't control us; she hadn't a clue.

—Fuck off hittin' me!

Gus Kinsella yelled that after she'd hit him on the loaf with her duster. She had her own duster that she brought everywhere with her. We said it was her Christmas present from her boyfriend. The boys had a different version; it was for wiping her arse and keeping her gee dry — she only used it as a duster because she needed the chalk. She should have walked out of the room and gone down to the headmaster when Gus Kinsella said that. She should just have walked out. She would have terrified us, especially Gus Kinsella; he was far worse than Derek O'Leary. She didn't, though. She was too scared. She was trapped. She couldn't report on us because she'd have been reporting on herself. It was the same for all of them. She was a hopeless poor clown. She was better than Brylcream-head, though.

34

That school made me rough. I wasn't like that before I started there.

—There's a smell of shite off yeh.

I never said anything like that before; I don't think I ever did. Now I had to act rough and think dirty. I had to fight. I had to be hard. Maybe it all happens anyway when you're growing up, no matter where you are; I don't really know. My John Paul was a little angel until about three days after his thirteenth birthday; Nicola didn't change in any way that was sudden or obvious, so I don't know. But it all started happening to me the minute I walked into that kip. Waters and his wandering thumb and Dillon and his wandering snot made me feel filthy; there was something about me that drew them to me, that made them touch me. It was my tits that I was too young for; I'd no right to them. It was my hair. It was my legs and my arms and my neck. There were things about me that were wrong and dirty. I thought that then; I felt it. I didn't say it to anybody; I wouldn't have known how to and I wouldn't have wanted to. I was a dirty slut in some way that I didn't understand and couldn't control; I made men and boys do things. I used to smell myself to see if it was that, some sort of a scent that I could wash off and they'd leave me alone and it could all go back to normal. There was no smell and it never did go back to normal.

—Fuck off.

—Fuck off.

—Fuck off, yourself.

—Fuck off.

Day in, day out.

—Get your fuckin' hands off me.

—Do your own fuckin' homework.

35

—Give that back, yeh cunt yeh.

I wasn't the only one. It happened to all of us. We went in children and we turned into animals. I don't blame Derek O'Leary. He was just a fast learner. By the end of the first week the class was full of Derek O'Learys, boy ones and girl ones.

—Fuck off.

—Fuck off.

—Fuck off.

All it took was someone leaning over and taking someone else's pencil, or someone sitting in too near to someone else. Or someone's head getting in the way of the blackboard. It took nothing.

—Fuck off.

—Fuck off.

—Fuck off.

I got pawed and I scraped back. I got scraped and I bit. I went home one dinner-time and I spent ages in the bathroom washing blood from under my fingernails. I remember being afraid that my mammy would come up. I was afraid that I'd have to explain it to her, explain it all, right back to the beginning. I don't think she ever noticed that I'd become different. At first, I tried to hide. I dragged my jumper down at the front, at the neck, so it would sag and make me disappear. Then I just gave up.

—What're you fuckin' lookin' at?

—Fuck off.

It wasn't all bad. It can't have been. There were the breaks at eleven and dinner-time. There was Fiona. There was something about her; you felt bigger just being with her. I changed my mind about her; I really liked her. We sat beside each other when we could.

—Get back to your proper place, Fiona Phillips, now.

36

—No.

—I beg your pardon.

—I want to sit here.

—I'm going to the headmaster.

—Yeah, you are; I dare yeh.

Fiona was a great combination, quick and lazy. She just had a way about her; she was sexy and she didn't care. A few years later I saw men drooling at her — their mouths hung open — and she didn't give a damn. She stood up to Dillon.

—Move over now, Miss Phillips; come on, push push.

—There's no room, said Fiona.

—Make room, come on.

—No.

Dillon was beaten. He couldn't do anything to Fiona. He could give her a bad Christmas report but she didn't care. Her parents couldn't read and she could get her older brother to lie when he was reading it for them. He couldn't hit her. She'd have hit him back and then the real trouble would have started. It was great. There wasn't a squeak in the room.

—You're getting fat, Miss Phillips.

That was the best he could do.

—Not as fat as you, said Fiona.

I had good friends, a whole gang of us. School finished at four o'clock. There were the breaks. There were laughs. There were free classes when the teachers were out pretending to be sick. We never had the full day's worth of teachers. We just stayed in the room and screamed and wrecked the place and each other and no one came near us. I'd go into a corner with Fiona and we'd chat for hours. We loved The High Chaparral. I liked Blue Boy and she liked Monolito. We used to argue about them. She was mad about

Mono. We nearly hit each other. (I've seen High Chaparral a couple of times on Sky in the afternoon and Fiona was right; Mono is much better looking than Blue Boy. Mono would nail you to the bed but poor oul' Blue Boy wouldn't know where to start. I didn't think that way then, when I was thirteen. I wouldn't object to teaching Blue Boy a thing or two now. It would fill some of those long afternoons and I'd be a better teacher than any of those useless cunts from the tech.)

It didn't even have a name. The primary school was called Saint Mary's. The tech was just the tech. The convent where the snobs went was called Holy Rosary. The brainy ones in primary were told to do the entrance exam for Holy Rosary. No one ever told me.

I tried — just now — to remember all the names of the other people in my class but I couldn't do it. I couldn't come near it. I hate when that happens. I can remember that it was raining the morning I started but I can't remember the names of the people who sat behind me. No such problem with the name of the little prick that sat beside me.

—What'll we call him if it's a boy?
—Not Derek.
—What?

I'm nearly certain that it started raining when I was waiting in the yard.

There was one poor fella in the class who'd had some sort of a terrible accident; his face was destroyed. It was red raw and white, he had no eyebrows; his whole face was warped. The skin was tight and horribly smooth. No hair grew until about an inch over his ear on one side; the skin there was the whitest thing I've ever seen. He'd pulled a chip pan down on himself

38

when he was small; that was the story. He never spoke unless he was made to. Then there was a gap — always there was — before he answered, as if it was taking all his strength to get the words out. I remember him exactly — I could draw him — but not his name. I hated it that he was in our class. He was the proof that we were nearly the worst, one step above retarded. At the same time I wanted to help him. I used to smile at him, but not in a way that would make him think I fancied him; I practised smiling at home. I can't remember his fuckin' name.

I changed. I noticed it then; I'm not just looking back. I changed. I stopped trying to hide myself. I pushed myself forward.

—What're you fuckin' lookin' at?

—Nothin' much.

—Fuck off.

I hated using bad language and then I stopped thinking about it. Derek O'Leary tried to feel me and I felt him back. I didn't squeeze; I just grabbed. He squirmed out of the seat onto the floor. He couldn't believe it; he was devastated.

—There's some of your own fuckin' medicine.

—Get off the floor, Derek O'Leary!

He couldn't say anything.

I grabbed him regularly from then on, what would now be called pre-emptive strikes. (I watched all the Gulf War stuff with Charlo. He loved that war.) I kept Derek O'Leary on his toes. He never enjoyed it. He left a nice big space between me and him. I had power, the only time in my life. I could make boys squirm. I tested it.

—Pick that up.

Two of them tried to get there first. I didn't thank

them. I practised my smiles. I looked over my shoulder into the mirror. I stared at my tongue; I licked my teeth. I held my hair over my head and let it fall and turned.

Are you the girl with the shining hair?

I wanked a boy in the back of the room. During Religion, in third year. Martin Kavanagh, one of the few fine things in the school and the only one in our class. Big and as thick as day-old shite. He was a big Slade fan. I didn't masturbate him: I wanked him. There's a difference, I think. During Religion. They all knew we were doing it; that was the point. No one looked, except Fiona; they were all scared of Martin. I'm left handed. I wrote down the list of the Holy Days of Obligation with my left hand and wanked him with my right. We changed places so I could do it. He can't have enjoyed it. The desks were very low; we were much too big for them by third year. My hand kept knocking the bottom of the desk. It was the first time I'd done it. I didn't look. His thing was hot and all of it seemed to be in my fist. I just wanted to get it done with before the bell went. Up down, up down; my fist went over him and walloped the desk. I grabbed him again. Up down — I could feel his trousers, the zip and the material. It must have been agony for him after a while. I looked at his face. He was gawking at the blackboard, biting his lip. He wouldn't look at me. His knees whacked the desk, then his legs shot out straight, under the desk in front of us.

—Neeaaa!

—Who made that noise?

I felt him coming. It terrified me. I didn't know what was happening. I thought it would scald me, it seemed so hot. I hadn't expected it. What colour was it? He pushed my hand away. He got his trousers back shut.

The hotness had gone off his come. It was cold now, so fast. I wouldn't look. I bent down and wiped the inside and outside of my hand on my sock, and hoped. I knew it wasn't blood; I knew that much. I don't know where the rest of it went, on the floor or the desk or the back of the fella in front of him. I never looked.

The bell went. Everybody knew.

I did it to him; he didn't do it to me. I did it.

My First Wank.

I was proud. I was a woman.

—What was it like?

—Lovely.

I'd survived.

I was someone.

I went with him for two weeks. I had to. You couldn't just wank a fella for the sake of it; you had to love him. I didn't do it again. He didn't ask me.

I'm a sucker for romance. If only it had been on a beach somewhere, or even a park. If only Martin had looked into my eyes. If he'd only had a brain. There was a map of the world on the wall behind us. Someone had drawn tits and a gee on South America. I wiped my hand on my sock. Really, you shouldn't have to wipe your hand at all. Here comes Robert Redford and his picnic rug again.

One thing for certain: I wouldn't have done it if I'd gone to the Holy Rosary. And I don't think I'd have done it if I'd been in 1.1. But my name was called out just when it started to rain and I ended up wanking a good-looking thick in the back of the classroom. That was how you made a name for yourself in 1.6.

10

Me then.

The girl who wanked Martin Kavanagh was five foot
three inches tall. Her sister had measured her. She had
brown hair, long and straight. Her ambition was to be
able to sit on it. She had good skin; there was never
any acne in her family. She had woman's legs; the little
girl was gone out of them. She had a scar just over her
left knee where her brother had stabbed her. She had
a thirty-four-inch bust. Bust was a normal word in
those days. She had brown eyes and people always
commented on her smile. She had shaved her legs three
times so far. She knew she was stupid but she didn't
mind that much. She didn't want to be a teacher any
more. She wanted to be an air hostess or an actress.
But any job would do her. Her mother said she was
nice enough looking to be a model but she had a
crooked tooth so she knew she couldn't be one. She
wanted to be a singer too, in a band; the only girl in it.
She'd sit on a stool for the slow songs. She knew all the
words of American Pie from start to finish. And Vincent. She sat on the windowsill in her bedroom when
she sang Vincent. She hated her school but she was
happy. She was glad she'd wanked Martin Kavanagh.
She was ashamed of herself and proud. She was someone. She was leaving school in a few months, after her
Group Cert. She was going to stroll through it. She
had her whole life ahead of her.

Me now.

The woman who masturbated Charlo Spencer is five feet four inches tall but she's been stooping a bit lately, her sister tells her. She still has brown hair, with a bit of help from something out of a bottle. She looks good if she remembers to stand up straight and you don't look at her too closely. People look but never too closely. Her arse is sagging a bit but she's the only one alive who knows. The skin of her face is veined, thin lines joining like tiny pink rivers on a map. They're easy to hide. She'll be thirty-nine in two months' time. Give her a mirror, some make-up and a half-hour and she'll make herself look thirty. See her when she's getting out of bed and she'll look fifty. She's an office cleaner; she gets two-fifty an hour. She does houses as well in the mornings. She's on an agency list but she doesn't have a phone. She has four children. She is a widow. She is an alcoholic. She has holes in her heart that never stop killing her. She sometimes thinks that she has cancer; she thinks that she deserves to have it. She isn't too fond of herself but she isn't so certain that she's stupid any more. She manages; she's a survivor. She has loose skin on her arms but her neck is still alright.

11

There was a pay phone in the takeaway. The Chinese girl behind the counter gave me her book. I looked under Coolock. I didn't know if that was the right station but it was where they'd usually brought Charlo when they'd wanted to have one of their chats with him. There was nothing on that page, only the Credit Union and the petrol station. I tried Garda; nothing there either. I knew that there was no point in going to S for Station. There was 999 but I didn't want to do that; what would I say?

I found it, in the green part at the front of the book. There was a list of all the Dublin stations. There were dozens of them. Coolock. Public Office — 8480811. There were three or four people in the takeaway waiting for their food.

—Hello. Coolock Garda Station.

They were quick; it hadn't even rung once.

—Is Gerard there?

—What? Coolock Garda Station.

—Is Gerard there?

—Gerard who?

—I don't know his other name; he's a Guard.

—Is he a young lad?

—Yes, I said.

—Looks a bit like Buster Keaton?

—Yes.

—Hang on till I see.

I heard laughing and a typewriter. Footsteps and someone singing. I'm leaving on a jet plane. Don't know. If I'll be back again. Then Good man, Gerard and more laughing.

—Hello?

—Is that Gerard?

—Yes.

—This is Paula, I said. —Missis Spencer.

—Hello, Missis Spencer, he said, loud enough for them all to hear.

—What happened him, Gerard?

—He said nothing.

—How did he die? You never told me.

44

—God — ; I'm sorry —
—It's alright. I should've asked.
—I forgot —
—It's alright.
There was no laughing now, or typing.
—He was — . He was shot.
—Was he?
—Yes. One of us — . Special Branch.
—Thanks, Gerard. I just wanted to know.
—He was armed, said Gerard.
I didn't want to hear any more; there was no room.
—He killed a woman.
—Who killed a woman?
—Mister Spencer.
—Okay.
—It'll be on the News.
—Okay; bye. Thanks.
—Bye.

12

I stopped being a slut the minute Charlo Spencer started dancing with me. I'll never forget it. People looked at me and they saw someone different.

Where I grew up — and probably everywhere else — you were a slut or a tight bitch, one or the other, if you were a girl — and usually before you were thirteen. You didn't have to do anything to be a slut. If you were good-looking; if you grew up fast. If you had a sexy walk; if you had clean hair, if you had dirty hair. If you wore platform shoes, and if you didn't. Anything could get you called a slut. My father called me a slut the first time I put on mascara. I had to go back up to the bathroom and take it off. My tears had ruined it anyway. I came back down and he inspected me.

—That's better, he said.

Then he smiled.

—You don't need it, he said.

My mother stayed out of it.

Carmel was always fighting with him. I remember the screams and the punches. She remembers them as well but she refuses to remember anything else, the good things about home and my father. It was hard for her, I know; she was the oldest and she had to fight all our fights. Fights — Jesus, they were wars. He tore clothes off her. He set fire to a blouse she'd bought with her first pay money. He dragged her up to the bathroom. He washed her face with a nailbrush. He locked her in our bedroom. He went after her when she got out. He took his belt to her in front of all her friends. He put me and Denise up on his knees and did horsey-horsey — it was embarrassing; I was much too old — while he stared at Carmel. He said that we were his girls, his great girls. He made Carmel go to the kitchen and make the tea; he told my mother to stay where she was.

—It's for her own good, he said when Carmel was gone.

She nodded. She agreed with him even though she was shaking. I remember being terrified. Denise looked from him to her, from him to her.

—Kettle on? he said when Carmel came back.

—Yeah.

—Good girl.

He loved her. That was why he did it. Fathers were

46

different then. He'd meant it for the best, being cruel to be kind. Carmel hated him. She remembers nothing else. She got married when she was seventeen.

—I'd have married anyone to get out of that house, she says. — I'd have married any invalid that asked me.

She got pregnant.

—Best thing I ever did.

Then got married.

My brother, Roger, called me a slut when I wouldn't let him feel me. I was fourteen; he was twelve. It was dark, in the kitchen. I thought it was a joke at first; he was my little brother. I'd gone in for a drink of water. He followed me. He put his hand up my skirt. I waited for him to tickle me. But it didn't happen. He was grabbing me. I thumped him.

—That hurt, I said.

I still thought he was messing.

—That hurt, I said again.

He tried to grab me again.

—Come on, he said.

Jesus, I don't know how many times I heard those words over the next few years. Come on. It never stopped. Come on. You were a slut if you let fellas put their tongues in your mouth and you were a tight bitch if you didn't — but you could also be a slut if you didn't. One or the other, sometimes both. There was no escape; that was you. Before I was a proper teenager, before I knew anything about sex, before I'd even left primary school — I was a slut. My daddy said it, fellas said it, other girls said it, men in vans and lorries said it. My mammy called me in off the street.

—You're getting too old, she said. —You'll get a name.

I helped her with the ironing. I liked being with her.

I put the clothes and bed things in the hotpress when she was finished ironing them. She was good at making you feel necessary.

I began to learn. It was alright to sit or lean on the wall during the day but not when it began to get dark. It wasn't respectable. Sitting on a wall in the dark would get you a name for yourself. You were looking for trouble, parading yourself, making a show of yourself. Getting yourself a bad name. Dying for it.

Smoking was another one. It was alright for a gang of girls to smoke, share the fag, laugh and cough. But it wasn't on for a young one to smoke by herself, say, to walk down the road by herself, smoking. She had the makings of a slut if she did that. Keeping the cigarette in her mouth when she was talking, that made her a definite slut. Smoking Major, the strongest, made her an absolute prostitute. If you didn't smoke at all you were tight and dry and a Virgin Mary.

Everything made you one thing or the other. It tired you out sometimes. I remember spending ages exhausted and upset. It was nice knowing that boys wanted you but then you couldn't want them back. If you smiled at more than one you were a slut; if you didn't smile at all you were a tight bitch. If you smiled at the wrong boy you were back to being a slut and you might get a hiding from his girlfriend, and she'd be a slut for pulling your hair and you'd be one for letting her. Boys could ask you to go with them and you couldn't ask them. You had to get your friends to let the boys know that you'd say yes if you were asked. That could make you a slut as well, if you got the wrong friend to ask for you. And then there were periods and keeping them secret and never mentioning them and making sure that no one knew and checking to make sure that there was no smell off you and — every day, every day — staying in the toilet till it was properly flushed and the water was clean again and, Jesus, if you went wrong once you were a slut.

—Slut.

My little brother.

—Slut.

My father.

—Slut.

Everyone. They were all in on it.

But it stopped when I started going with Charlo. God, it was great. I could have walked around in my nip with twenty Major in my mouth combing my pubic hair and nobody would have said a word. I was Charlo's girl now and that made me respectable. Men kept their mouths shut when I went by. They were all scared of Charlo and I loved that. It was like revenge. I could have pointed out fellas to Charlo, told him to kill them and he would have. And they knew it. And I knew it. I was a good fighter myself; I could crease any young one that ever got in my way. But being a good fighter made no difference; you were still only a girl and a slut. As far as fellas were concerned, being good in a fight only made you an even bigger slut. They laughed at girls fighting even though they were scared; girls fought to maim and kill. Girls didn't box. Girls tore flesh off and tried to blind each other. Girls knew the importance of hair. Most boys didn't really fight at all; girls always did. Boys pretended; girls didn't. Boys pretended that girls couldn't fight and everybody believed them. I was a great fighter. Nobody cared.

Charlo could fight like a girl. Charlo didn't go by the rules because when he was fighting he didn't know them, he wasn't thinking. Not till the end of a fight, when he stopped and started planting his kicks, then he was thinking about it; that was when it became really vicious and bad. But he didn't fight much. He didn't have to. One look at Charlo told fellas that they were dead if he felt like it. All I had to do was point.

He walked me home the first night. All the way to my house. Guitar Man followed My Eyes Adored You and Charlo didn't let go of me. His head moved. I looked up and his mouth was there and I opened mine before his got there so he'd see it and know that I wanted to kiss him. I could taste the smoke and the drink and I could nearly swear that he'd had egg and chips for his tea, but it was great. We looped the loop and wore the faces off each other till the end of the song and the D.J. changed the record — he only had one turntable. We both stopped at the exact same time.

—What's your name? he said.

—Paula, I said. —What's yours?

—Charlo Spencer, he said.

His fringe came down over his eyebrows.

—Have you heard of me?

—No, I said. —Is that short for Charles?

—Yeah, he said.

—Does your ma call you that as well? I said.

—Yeah, he said.

He looked at me; he wasn't sure if I was slagging him. I surprised myself sometimes when I was cheeky. I didn't plan it.

—I like your jacket, I said.

He put his hand on it.

—It's nice, I said.

(—What was Tony wearing when you first saw him? I asked Nicola.

Tony is her fella, a lovely kid.

—I don't know, she said. —Somethin'; it was ages ago, sure; years. His uniform, I think. I can't remember.

—Well, I said. —You should try to remember these things.

—Why should I? she said.

—Because they become important later on, I said.

She looked at me; her forehead creased.

—I'm embarrassed for yeh, she said.

She sighed, the wagon, pretending she didn't want to ask me.

—What was my da wearin'?

—A stolen bomber jacket, I said.

—Stolen?

—Yeah. And Wrangler parallels.

—Parallels?

—Yep.

—What're *they*?

They.

I drew her a pair on a piece of paper.

—What colour was the jacket?

—Black.

—You've a great memory.

—It's easy to remember black, I said. —All the bomber jackets were black.

—Black's nice.

—Yeah. Not *all* black though. You need a bit of colour.

—What about his shoes? she said.

—Black as well.

—What type?

—Loafers.

—Jesus!

She laughed.

—With the tassels on them?

51

—Yeah.

She was starting to annoy me, just a teeny-weeny bit. I could see why parallels were funny but there was nothing wrong with loafers. They were still a good shoe.

—Jesus, she said.

It was my own fault for trying to include her. She's too young. She doesn't have a past yet. Mind you, that isn't true either. But her past is too close to her present. She has no need to look back yet. She has — and I really believe this — her whole life ahead of her.)

Charlo respected me, I have to say that. All the way home to St Francis Avenue. He didn't try to get his feel or pull me behind a wall or none of the usual stuff. It was nice for a change. We just walked. He didn't say much and most of it was boasting, but that's fellas for you. He was funny. He didn't mind me laughing. He stopped holding my hand whenever we were coming up to people and passing them. I asked him questions. He liked it. I asked if he'd ever been in jail. He was chuffed. I'd given it away; I knew all about him. He told me he'd been in St Pat's.

—For how long?

—Three months.

—Jesus. What was it like?

—Alright; not bad.

—It's not really jail though, is it? I said. —It's only for kids.

—It fuckin' is so jail, he said. —I was in a cell.

—On your own?

—Sometimes.

—I'd hate that, I said.

He'd been in for robbing. He'd been caught loads of times, shoplifting and with stuff out of stolen cars, mostly radios. Then they found him up on top of an old house in Kinsealy taking the lead off the roof, him and another fella. The old people in the house had phoned the Guards.

—We thought the place was empty, he said. —We made a huge hole in the fuckin' roof. Lovely bit of lead.

I asked him if he still robbed. He said he didn't. All kids robbed; they were wild and then they stopped when they grew up. They didn't need the buzz. He had a job. He was a builder. One of his little brothers was in Pat's now.

—The same cell?

—Don't know. He'll see my name if he is. I can't stand the little cunt.

(I hadn't met his family yet, of course. They were all robbers. It was in their blood. They robbed that as well, out of Pelican House.)

I loved that walk home. It was probably the best part of all the years with him, though maybe I'm just being stupid. It was warm and windy. I remember it well and I don't care if anyone can prove that it was raining, like the man on the Late Late Show who could prove that it was too cloudy for the moon to be out on the night Annie Murphy got ridden by the Bishop of Galway. It wasn't fuckin' raining; it was lovely. I wasn't a bit scared of him, or worried. After only ten minutes he was a friend; that was the way I felt — and I fancied him as well. I thought he was an absolute ride. I wouldn't have minded if he had pulled me behind a wall. But he didn't. He respected me. He'd do that to me later; I knew it would happen. I always knew what to expect. Fellas were like easy crosswords; you knew the answers before you'd finished the questions, and they usually weren't worth doing. But this was different. I liked the

53

idea that I was getting to know him, that I could already read him. It was different; it was perfect. I'm able to remember it without what came after, the bad years and the terrible years. Warm dry wind, his hand — dry as well — the manly clip of his heels, his smoke, his side-to-side walk. I began to walk like him so we wouldn't keep bashing into each other. They all walked like that then, the fellas. You can still see them now, in their forties and late thirties, walking like they're afraid they'll topple over because their balls are so heavy. We must have looked ridiculous, the pair of us, strolling through Brookwood like two hard penguins. I didn't feel a bit ridiculous then, though. I was walking with Charlo Spencer. He was holding my hand. He was taking me home. I was with Charlo Spencer. He was the King, and that made me someone. Not a Queen or a Princess, just someone. It was a start. It filled me. I could feel it in my walk.

13

—What went wrong with Daddy?
   —He was always like that.
   —No, he wasn't. He wasn't, Carmel.
   —He was, said Carmel.
   —He wasn't, I said. —Remember Courtown?
   —Yeah.
   —D'you remember, Denise?
   —Yeah. The caravan.
   —Wasn't it brilliant?

Carmel got there before Denise; she wouldn't let her answer.

—I remember Courtown alright, she said. —I remember fuckin' Courtown alright.

—Jesus, Carmel; back off.

—Why should I? she said. —I remember it as well. I know what you're fuckin' up to.

—Do you remember it, Denise? I said.

—Yeah, said Denise.

She was looking at Carmel; she was looking guilty. She didn't want to take sides. She was always Carmel's sidekick, her fuckin' Tonto.

—Wasn't he great then? I said.

—Yeah, said Denise.

She looked at Carmel.

—He was.

—Not just then, I said. —Every Sunday, we used to go out. Bray and Skerries. We always got chips and 99s.

—Jesus Christ, said Carmel.

—We did, Carmel, I said. —You can't say we didn't.

—So what? said Carmel. —For fuck sake; the two of you. Do you remember the times when we didn't want to go anywhere on Sunday? Do you remember what happened then? Do you remember what happened if you dropped your fuckin' 99? Well? D'you remember Mammy crying because she'd put too much vinegar on his chips, do yis? Ask her.

—He was nice then, I said.

—When it suited him.

—He was nice. At home. Watchin' the telly. We were always laughin'.

—Yeah yeah, maybe.

—What do you think, Denise? I said.

I felt sorry for her but she annoyed me as well, always

55

in the middle. Clueless and gutless. That isn't fair, but she can really get on my wick sometimes.

—I don't know, she said.

But I gave her more time because I knew that she was only starting; she was making her mind up, taking the plunge.

—Yes, he was nice.

Jesus, I felt good. That proved it, what Denise had just said; I wasn't just making it all up. My stomach landed and took off. I felt secure. I felt sane. It's a valuable feeling. It's a long time since I took it for granted.

Denise confirmed it. The man I remembered was my father. I wasn't wasting my time or fooling myself. Once upon a time my life had been good. My parents had loved me. The house was full of laughter. I'd run to school every morning.

Carmel wasn't finished. She went for Denise. (Not really, Paula; be fair.) She looked at Denise — hard — and spoke to her.

—All the time?

—No, said Denise. —Who's nice all the time? I'm not sayin' he was a fuckin' saint, Carmel.

Carmel was shocked. Denise had answered her back, probably for the first time ever. Denise was enjoying it.

—He was nice, she said. —He sang a lot, didn't he?

—So did Hitler.

—Ah stop, Carmel, will yeh, I said. —Is that the best you can do?

—I know what you're up to, she said.

—What?

—I know.

—What?

—Rewriting history, she said.

—I don't know what you're talkin' about, I said. —I don't even know what you mean.

—I'm sure you have your reasons, said Carmel.

—Fuck off, Carmel, will yeh.

(I'm not. What Carmel says. Rewriting history. I'm doing the opposite. I want to know the truth, not make it up. She has her reasons too.)

—It's my house, said Carmel. —You fuck off.

She glared at Denise.

—The two of you.

She didn't mean it. She filled our glasses. Denise was a bit shaky; I saw it when she was picking up her glass. She was coming down after her rush.

—It's not just Daddy, said Carmel. —All men are the same. Basically bastards.

—Ah no, I said.

I didn't know if I really disagreed with her; I wasn't sure. But Carmel said things too easily, and got away with them.

—They can't be.

—They are, said Carmel. —Basically. I think.

—Not really.

—Yeah, said Carmel. —Even the nice ones.

—Yeah, said Denise.

That annoyed me. She was licking up to Carmel.

—No, I said. —What about your Harry? He's a lovely man.

(I didn't believe that; I think her Harry's a boneless little drip.)

—He can be a bastard as well, said Denise. —You're not with him all the time.

—Ah, for fuck sake, I said. —You can say that about anybody, not just men.

—Maybe, said Carmel. —You might be right.

—I'm not drinkin' gin any more, said Denise.

—Don't blame the drink, love, said Carmel.

—I'm not, said Denise. —I'm just goin' to start cryin' and I don't want to. And now I do.

—Jesus.

—Listen, I said. —I lived for twenty years. Nearly twenty, with a bastard. The bastard of all fuckin' bastards. I know one when I see one. Will you give me that?

—No problem, said Carmel.

—All men are not bastards, I said.

—Name one that isn't, said Carmel.

—Okay.

—Off you go; come on.

—Okay, I said. —Jesus, I think I'm drunk.

—Don't start, said Carmel. —Name one. Go on.

—Nicola's fella; Tony.

—He's lovely, said Denise.

—He's only a kid, said Carmel. —He'll learn.

—He's lovely, I said. —Isn't he, Denise?

—Yeah.

—Robert Redford, I said.

—Him! said Carmel. —Did you see him in that last one? It was on the Movie Channel. He bought your woman for a million dollars.

—Indecent Proposal, said Denise.

—He was a right fuckin' creep in it anyway.

—That wasn't him, I said. —He was only acting.

—I wouldn't pay a tenner for that bitch. Who's that she's married to again?

—Bruce Willis.

—Now there's a bastard.

—Charlo liked him.

—Jesus.

I went home happy. I lay in bed happy. I rarely felt like that, unless Jack or Leanne came into me and cuddled up against me and I could hear them sleeping and knew that they needed me. This was different, nothing to do with love or the kids or being wanted. It was about me. I felt solid. I wasn't drunk. I didn't really get drunk in the old way any more. My head was clear. I was wide awake; it was way past midnight. I felt solid. I felt right. I'd got something right. I could trust my memory. My father was my father; my past was my past. I could start again. I could believe myself. The things that came into my head were true. My father had been a nice man. Charlo had been a loving husband. I had been a good-looking woman. It hadn't always been like this. I had once been a girl. I used to read my stories out in class. I used to drink only at the weekends. My hair was nearly long enough for me to sit on. I believed it when I prayed; I really thanked O Lord for the food he gave me. Men whistled. I had a lovely smile. I practised it but it came natural. I cooked great Sunday dinners. I made Bisto my own. Charlo peeled the spuds and carrots. I lay in my cot and the wind lifted the curtains and dropped them. All these things were in my head and all of them were true. Just a few words from Denise. He was nice. Proof. My past was real. I could stand on it and it wouldn't collapse under me. It was there.

I could start again.

Men whistled.

Daddy laughed.

My husband peeled the spuds.

14

They were out on the street — Carmel had run them out of the garden — waiting for anything to happen, journalists and photographers and just people, neighbours and people who had just come to see the house. But I didn't know anything about them. I was in the kitchen. I didn't move. Jack's picture was in all the papers the day after, Jack looking out the window. Jack is five. He's the most beautiful child I've ever seen. He makes me cry, just looking at him.

—He killed a woman.

That was all I knew about it.

—It'll be on the News.

—Okay; bye. Thanks.

—Bye.

I hadn't seen the News. I wasn't interested. My mouth had gone numb on me. I weighed a ton. All I was good for was tea, vodka and sitting in the kitchen. They put soup in front of me but I couldn't manage it. It was too full, too packed; I couldn't have swallowed it.

I'd made it home easily enough. I didn't think. I didn't feel. I walked. I divided the journey into pieces, seven corners, four roads to cross. Past the pub, the car park and the bus shelter, the shop-van, the dry cleaners, the church. Past O'Neill's house, Mooney's, O'Connor's. The green, the pitch, the subway. I didn't look at anything.

It would be on the News.

I made it. I had my key ready, straight in, no shakes. I was home. The house was still empty. I was alone. Then I wasn't. Carmel and Denise were there. I was on the floor. They picked me up.

—Paula, love —

They hugged me. Next, I was in the kitchen.

—It's freezin' in here; Jesus.

—She needs heat or she'll go into shock.

—I'm alright, I said.

—Sit down there, said Carmel. —Do nothing.

—It's your day off, said Denise.

—Don't overdo it, Denise, said Carmel.

I sat and they surrounded me.

—Now, said Carmel.

She put a mug of tea in front of me.

—Loads of sugar in it.

—Thanks.

Then she put the bottle on the table.

—Thanks very much.

—No problem.

I threw the vodka in on top of the tea.

—Good girl.

It was a new mixture. I liked it.

—He's dead, I said.

—That's right, said Carmel.

Nothing else.

—*I'll* tell Nicola, I said.

—Okay.

—When she comes in.

—Okay.

—When she comes in.

—Yeah.

—She has a job, I said.

I don't know what made me say that, and I remember that I definitely did say it. I wanted to tell Nicola. She was older than me in some ways. She'd an old mind inside her lovely head. I didn't know if it was strength or deformity; when I was feeling low I felt guilty about

61

it. I was to blame for it; I'd robbed her and crippled her. I was proud of her. She stunned me sometimes. I'd made a right hash of my life but she wasn't going to. It wasn't that she could find work or that she was beautiful — all my kids are beauts — it was her shrug. She'd shrug past the Charlos and the bastards. She'd never become an alco like her mother. She'd never look fifty until she was fuckin' fifty, and then she'd probably look forty. Nicola was something else. There were some times when I was so jealous I wanted to maim her, really hurt her. I adored her. She was my pride and joy; still is.

Jack and Leanne had the telly on loud and Denise had the hoover out — she's always loved hoovers — and some of her and Carmel's kids were floating around as well but I heard nothing except the click of the door.

Nicola was home.

Half-six.

She knew. She'd walked past all the houses along the way. She might have seen faces in the windows; one or two that I know would definitely have been gawking out at her going past. She'd have seen all the journalists. She'd have put on her face, her I-never-smiled-in-my-life face, as she got nearer. They'd have seen her and guessed that she was Charlo's daughter. There'd have been a stampede. They might have pushed her when she was getting past them. Click click, the cameras. She'd have pushed them back. They'd have got out of her way, if they knew what was good for them. She'd have heard the cameras clicking and whirring as she was opening the door. She'd have seen the flashes behind her —

—Miss Spencer —

—Nicola; this way this way —

—Miss Spencer—

She wouldn't have looked back.

The picture in the Herald showed her almost smiling, her shoulder lifted as if to protect herself. It didn't do her justice.

All I heard was the click of the door.

Carmel led her into the kitchen to me. She held the lapels of her jacket like it was cold and windy.

—Your daddy's dead, love.

I didn't even stand up. My legs weren't up to it.

—Oh.

She shrugged. I knew she would; I'd put mental money on it. There was so much in that shrug. I leaned over and grabbed her. I pressed the side of my face into her stomach and wouldn't let go. I cried. I hoped that she'd cry — she needed to, I wanted her to cry. I wanted to think that she needed me. I wanted her to hold my head. I could hear her tummy grumbling.

Carmel got my arms apart and rescued poor Nicola.

—How? she said.

I wiped my eyes. Carmel was waiting to see if I'd answer.

—Shot, I said.

Now I shrugged.

We all started laughing.

—Shot, I said it again. —Can you believe it?

We were still laughing. Denise closed the kitchen door so the kids outside couldn't hear us; it wouldn't have sounded proper. It was a bit indecent, laughing at the way your husband had got himself killed. We all had to wipe our eyes. I noticed that. Even Carmel.

—The police, I told Nicola.

She nodded.

—We can watch it on the News, I said.

Her forehead creased, the way it does.

—Did they film it?

—What? No, no. I meant just the news about it; it'll be on.

15

His mother looked me up and down like she was thinking of buying me. I stood on the back step. Charlo went ahead of me.

—That's Paula, he said, and he rushed through the kitchen into the hall and left me there on the step with the dark behind me and his fuckin' mother in front of me. And I was half-pissed and there was no escape. He'd gone to the jacks. It was the only thing that ever made him hurry.

—I'm fuckin' burstin', he'd said just before he opened the back door. It hadn't stopped him from grabbing my arse when we were going through his alley to the back. I'd screamed. I was bursting as well, and cold. Someone had robbed my jacket. His mother must have heard me.

—Hello, I said.

I said Hello and not Howyeh. All mothers said that their sons' girlfriends were common. My mammy said it about Roger and Eddie's girlfriends. All the mothers were the same. I was drunk as a skunk, I'd no jacket on me, there was probably grass on my back, I was smiling crooked but I made sure I said Hello instead of Howyeh.

—Come in, she said.

64

—Thanks very much, I said.

She was making sandwiches. For Charlo's da and his brothers. They were all in watching the telly. I was never certain how many brothers Charlo had. There were sisters as well. They were easier to count; there were three of them. The three fuckin' pigs. I watched her buttering the bread. She was the only person I ever knew who could manage butter straight from the fridge. It was great to watch.

—Shut the door there.

I couldn't manage it.

—You have to lift it.

I tried but it wouldn't shut for me. I thought I was going to piss.

—Here.

She shoved me out of the way, her elbow right into my side. She put her two hands under the knob and groaned and carried the door in the last half-inch. The latch clicked.

—One of them lazy gets in there will fix it one of these days.

I leaned where I'd landed when she'd shoved me and waited for Charlo to come back down and rescue me. She slapped slices of ham down onto the bread; I could hear the air escaping from under the meat. The kitchen was smaller than ours at home. The ceiling was lower and slanting down towards the back door. It was stuck on to the back of the house, not really a proper part of it; you had to go up two uneven cement steps to get into the house itself. There was the smell of dinners and teas. When she'd finished piling the sandwiches — they were like a block of flats — she held them down like they were trying to escape and sliced through them with one lunge of the bread knife. Then she picked up the plate and walked the few steps over to the wall opposite. She pulled back a curtain that I hadn't really noticed. There was a big window behind it. The sitting room was behind that and they were all in there watching the telly; I could see the backs of the tops of their heads and Charlo was in there too, the fucker. She knocked on the glass and an older version of Charlo stood up, opened the window and took the plate off her. He shut the window, leaned out to haul it back in.

She closed the curtain. She was big. She reminded me of an Indian woman or a knacker, the same huge soundless way of moving. She knew exactly where everything was, even things that had no fixed place. A knife on the table — her hand went out and took it up by the handle while she was turning on the cold tap and facing the sink. Her shoulders were massive. There was no fat there under her dress; it was all strength. The dress was flowery but there were no real colours. Her hair was black and grey and long, the longest I'd ever seen on a middle-aged woman. It wasn't tied up or anything. It was loose. She'd shake her head to get it out of the way, and it obeyed. She was like a statue, big and solid; there was something magnificent about her. But I could see it as well — she was bad. She hated things.

The kettle was colossal. She swung it and landed it on the gas. She turned and looked over at me. There was only a yard between us.

—D'you drink tea?

—Yes.

I didn't know if I was going to get any. Charlo was a bollox for dumping me there; either he thought we'd be having a chat or he didn't give a shite. He knew his mother; she didn't chat — she wasn't interested.

—D'you have a name?

—Yes. —— Paula.

—That's right: he told me.

Her name was Gert but I only found that out after. When I asked Charlo he wasn't sure; he had to think about it.

She had the teapot now. She came towards me. For a second I thought she was going to skull me with it. She threw the lid on the table. She got the doorknob and choked it open. She threw what was left in the pot out the door into the yard. I heard water landing on cement. She stepped back and lifted the door shut.

—One of them will fix it some day.

—Where's the toilet?

—Upstairs.

—Thanks.

I escaped, up the two steps into the house. It was brighter. The sound from the room to the right was a film — gunfire — and all the men talking about it. I went past to the stairs and up. I had everything I'd ever drunk crying to get out of me. I bent a bit to make it easier to carry. It was dark at the top, no lights on, no switch that I could see. I could make out doors. One of them looked open. I gave it a shove and hooshed my skirt up; it was dribbling out of me now. I got in, found the switch, turned on the light; it was a bedroom and there was a man lying on one of the beds. And my knickers were heading down over my knees before I realised.

—Oh Jesus!

He was awake, lying back. He'd lifted his head.

—Sorry, I said.

The insides of my legs were wet; I couldn't get my knickers back.

67

—No problem, he said. —Next door.

His head fell back.

I turned the light off.

—Thanks, he said.

I wouldn't make it; all I wanted now was to get onto lino. I kept my skirt right up at my waist. I got to the next door, shoved in, turned on the light, saw the bath, and I emptied. I looked down; lino.

—Thank God.

It was the longest piss I've ever had, and the loudest. I could hear nothing else. I'll never forget it. I didn't go again for days after; I couldn't. And I never drank cider again.

I'd saved my skirt; it was dry. I used up most of the toilet paper wiping the floor. I left some. There was only one towel, a dirty white one. I used it to wipe the rest of the floor, then I rinsed it and hung it on the side of the bath. I flushed the toilet and prayed to Mary that it wouldn't clog. It took ages before I was convinced that all the paper was going to be taken. I rinsed my knickers. But I had nowhere to put them. I'd no pockets; my jacket had been robbed. I didn't want to chance the toilet; I could see them floating there flush after flush and me waiting for the cistern to fill again and listening for one of the brothers coming up the stairs, or the father or the mother — there was no way.

I threw them out the window. I didn't care; I just wanted to get rid of them. They were wet and heavier than they should have been so I think they went well into the garden, maybe even over the back wall. I listened for them landing but I heard nothing. A good pair they were too. I shut the window.

16

The first fella I ever went with, it was gas. I was only eleven. I went with him after he asked me. He had to ask me first though. It was all very formal, very proper. It was very like an engagement from the old days, only he didn't have to ask my father for my hand. That would have been really great, watching the poor little young fella — he was a little lad — knocking on the door and asking for my daddy.

I fancied him because he was two years older than me and he had nice clothes. There was a matching corduroy trousers and waistcoat outfit that I remember, halfway between brown and orange. The waistcoat fitted him so well that the sleeves of his shirt seemed to be part of it. There wasn't a crease, except the ones that were supposed to be there. He didn't have brothers or sisters and I liked that about him too. It seemed to make him more complete and unusual. Exotic. Intelligent. Sad. He had lovely fair hair, not too white, and he went a great colour in the summer. He had a frown that I loved, a single light wrinkle that went at a slant across his forehead; it was gorgeous. I used to annoy him just to see it, or ask him hard questions or embarrass him. I wanted to kiss it. I wanted to follow it with my tongue or my finger. His big toes looked at each other when he was standing still but he had a normal walk. I was only eleven but I could recognise a nice little bum when I saw one; you should have seen him in those cord trousers. He had a little tummy on him, a tummy you'd expect on a much younger boy, a milk tummy. It was strange because his face was quite old. The two parts didn't seem to fit. Then he turned around and you saw his bum and you got very confused; you began to feel guilty — even when you were only eleven. It was easier to look at him in instalments. Blue eyes, of course, with the fair hair. A lovely ridge on his top lip. A chin that stopped just before it could get pointy. His cheeks. His fringe. I remember all this. I remember all this but I can't remember his name. What is it about me and names?

Weirder still, I can't remember which house he lived in. I can't remember the road or the garden, the colour of the front door. Just to see if I could do it, I sat for a while on my own this morning when Jack was at school and I went from house to house along our road in my head, the road I lived on when I was a child, from our house to the corner, across the road, down the other side to the other corner, across and up, back to our house. I could remember all the names, all the people in each family. It was easy once I got started. I was delighted — I often wonder if my brain's gone, if I've wrecked it from drinking and living — but I felt incredibly sad too; I started bawling. All of those people, all of them happy. A mother and a father and their children. There was a dog in nearly every house. It seemed so lovely as I went from one side of the road to the other, I knew I was going to cry before I got to the end. I nearly wanted Carmel to come in and ruin it. And it seemed so long ago as well. And unreachable. And I started thinking about the road I live on now and the people all around me — the differences — and I knew that I wasn't the only one who'd been flushed down the toilet in the last twenty years. But it didn't make me feel any better. Even the dogs are different now. They're not pets any more; they don't know what they are. I missed all of those people, the neighbours;

the nice ones and the mad ones, the ones that drank and the ones that went to mass every day, the girls and boys and babies.

He must have lived around one of the corners because he wasn't in any of the houses on our road and he definitely lived near us. I'd never have gone with anyone from far away when I was eleven, and far away meant anything more than three minutes' walk. Anyway, I wanted to go with him. All my friends were doing it, going with fellas or talking about it. I wanted my turn. I wanted to hear me being talked about. My best friend, Dee, had gone with three fellas in three weeks; she broke it off three Sundays in a row. Fiona was the first one of us to bring back a love-bite. She only went with that fella for two days. The record was Mary O'Gorman. She told a fella she'd go with him, then she broke it off with him after half an hour.

—He was only after me jacket, she said.

She was a gas young one. It was a denim jacket; her big brother had given it to her when he didn't want it any more. He still wore it sometimes but it was hers; she let him.

—He asks me first, she said.

She wasn't really in our gang. We all liked her, but not enough to let her in. I don't think she minded. I'm not sure that she even noticed. I'd hate to think that we hurt her. I used to love meeting her years later, on the street or the bus — before I got married and moved away. She was hilarious. She didn't give a shite; she spoke out loud.

—His hands, Jesus; for a minute I thought I had three tits.

She'd have you in stitches. She was funny about everythin_

71

—The bus must be having a shite round that corner. I've been waiting here for fuckin' ages.

I loved meeting her but I never tried to get to know her better, even when the gang had broken up and gone — Dee to England, Fiona married. There was something about her. She didn't fit. I did. I preferred it that way. I was still happy. I think. I don't remember it any other way. (I'd love to meet her now. I think I'd recognise her. I don't think she'd recognise me. I don't know if I'd be able to stop her if she was walking past me.

—What have you been up to yourself? she'd say.

Where would I start?)

Anyway, my time had come. I wanted to go with someone. It couldn't be just any young fella; I had to pick the right one. There were loads of fellas to choose from. They poured out of every house every morning, hundreds of them. All the parents were the same age; all their children were the same age. There were hundreds of fellas my age. That was the first thing though: he had to be older, even just a bit. You couldn't have a toy-boy when you were only eleven. But if he was much older he'd say no. I knew I looked older than my age — people kept telling me and looking at me — but a fella two years older was the most I could get away with. Stephen Rooney was thirteen and dead nice but he was as ugly as sin, God love him. Saying hello to Stephen Rooney when there was anyone around to hear you was like having your skirt blown up and your knickers shown off to everyone; it was an instant redner and it lasted longer. Harry Quigley was beautiful but he was fourteen and too good-looking. Dee said that he'd done it with Missis Venison from beside the shops — her husband was in the British Navy — and it was

72

easy to believe. He was like a man already, a small, smooth man. His little brother, Albert, was gorgeous as well but he was only ten. He'd have been perfect; I could have just cuddled him and told him what clothes to wear and brought him around with me everywhere. But I'd never have lived it down.

—Baby snatcher.

—Where's his pram?

—Slut.

My head was full of fellas for days, real ones for a change; The Monkees didn't live on our road. I chose the one with the waistcoat because he was older than me — nearly two years — but small, not too much older, the same size. He wasn't really good-looking in the usual way. I was being realistic. There were parts of him that were absolutely gorgeous but not enough to make him that way overall. He was elegant. So was Charlo. I've always liked elegance, from the very start. Elegance in a man is a very rare thing, in an Irishman anyway, and especially in Dublin. Not so much the clothes, but the way they're worn. I've never liked really flashy clothes; that's not elegance. It's the way the clothes are worn, if they're clean and match, if they fit properly. You could spend your day walking around here before you'd see a man in a pair of trousers that fit him properly. Charlo always dressed well, even in just jeans and a t-shirt; he always looked well. Clothes say a lot; I've always thought that. (I dress like a knacker these days but that says something as well, I suppose. I used to make my mind up about what I'd wear every morning, before I got out of the bed. There was never much of a choice but I remember that it was part of my day. Now, I'm wearing an old pair of runners that Nicola didn't need when she left school three years ago and didn't have to do P.E. any more. And blue jeans that have no blue left in them and make my arse look bigger. But I still make an effort on Sundays. Or when I'm going out, which is just often enough to stop me from saying never. My sisters take me out sometimes and make me enjoy myself.) My first fella was an elegant little man. His mother made and bought his clothes and she might have put them on him but he was the one that wore them. He was straight-backed — another thing I've always liked; straight-backed Dublin men don't grow on trees either — and he never put his hands in his pockets. He swung his arms. A little soft army man. He was just right. There was a good chance that he'd say yes. I'd a feeling that I was good-looking enough, especially if he wasn't all that interested. I made my mind up and fell in love with him.

—D'yeh know —

What was his fuckin' name!

—I think he's lovely.

Dee was my best friend. She was going to be my messenger. I could trust her and I'd done it for her, gone up to one of her fellas and told him that she wanted to go with him. We were sitting on the back step of our house, just me and Dee. I was nervous. I might have made the wrong choice; I'd see it in Dee's face.

—Yeah, she said. —He's nice.

God, I was happy sitting there. It must have been a sunny day. It couldn't have been cold.

—I'd love to go with him, I said.

—Yeah, she said.

She didn't mean that she wanted to go with him too; she was just being nice.

—Will yeh tell him for me? I asked.

74

—Okay, she said.

I waited at the corner. She went up and told him. She came back.

—He says yeah.

I waited for him. Dee went to the shops to wait for me. He came over to me.

—Will you go with me?

—Yeah.

—Thanks.

Isn't that lovely? He said Thanks. I remember it. And that was it. I was going with him.

I went after Dee.

—What did he say?

—He said yeah.

—That's brilliant.

I went with him for eleven days, then I broke it off. We never kissed but that was alright; I was happy with that. We only met twice, but that was alright too. The thing was to be going with a fella, not to be with him all the time. You could go with a fella and not ever see him at all, it didn't matter. If you were going with him you were going with him. I broke it off because I wanted to. I just wanted to. I wanted to be able to say it. I wanted the word to go around; she broke it off with him. I wanted the power.

—Why are you breaking it off with him?

—I just am, right.

You had to get a friend to let the fella know that you wanted to go with him but you had to break it off yourself.

—I don't want to go with you any more; okay?

—Okay.

—We can still be friends.

—Okay.

—Seeyeh.
—Seeyeh.

It was easy.

I never spoke to him again. I had a little cry to myself that night but I really felt great. I could take a few risks now. It didn't matter as much if a fella said no; I'd already had one and blown him out, a nice one too. I could get a few notches on my belt.

I went with dozens of fellas after that for about a year. We swapped them around and they didn't know. They didn't really know what was going on. I suppose it made them feel good, being chased by little young ones. Sometimes it actually was like a game of chasing; you'd dump one and run after another. It was gas. Absolutely harmless. It was all playing, pretending, copying older people. I'd go into a field with one fella and sometimes we'd do absolutely nothing, not even talk; we'd stay a bit and go back to the rest. They'd nudge one another when we were coming towards them. I'd make myself blush.

We were still a bit young to be called sluts for it. Anyway, the young fellas all thought that they were in charge; they asked us to go with them — but they wouldn't have if we hadn't made them. There was no real kissing or feeling. It was all about ownership really. You had to have a fella. I went with nearly all the fellas the right age on our road. None of them said no. I even went with Bickies O'Farrell for a bit because I felt sorry for him. I went with him for an afternoon but I broke it off before I went home for my tea because I wanted to go with someone else after, when it was getting dark; I didn't want to waste the whole day. Poor Bickies. You had to be very careful what you shouted out in the street, even when you were only seven.

—I want bickies!

He was Bickies up until the day I got married and he was twenty-three then. Not a bad-looking young fella either, just a complete and utter eejit, so thick he couldn't control the expression on his face — that kind of fella.

We went with Barry Feeney, Dessie Feeney — twins — Fergie O'Toole, Francis Xavier Elliott, Kevin Harrison, Sean Williamson, Frano Grant, all of them — one day, two days. Three and half weeks was my record. That was with Martin Kearns. I was proud of that one; he'd said no to Dee and Fiona. He was a ride. I had to get Carmel to ask him.

—Do you remember?

—Yep.

—Which one was he? said Denise.

She's younger than us so there was a whole new batch of fellas on the road by the time she got round to it. I don't think she was much into fellas. Athletics was Denise's big thing. She ran a lot. Harry's about the only one she ever went with, and she married him. He was a runner as well, I think. She won a few cups and medals; I remember her taking them home and we got ice-cream to celebrate. I was on all sorts of diets by then. I wouldn't eat it. I wasn't being bitchy but Denise thought I was and so did my mother.

—Martin Kearns, I said. —He had brothers. He was nice.

—I remember it alright, said Carmel.

She sat up, the way she does when she's getting going.

—I was sixteen —

—You were not, I said.

—I was, she said. —I was working.

77

—I was only eleven, I told her. —So you could only have been fourteen. At the most.

—Listen, she said. —I'll tell my version and then you can tell your pack of lies. Anyway, Denise, this brasser here was waiting for me when I got home. *From work.*

—What work? I said.

—Shut up. She was waiting in the hall for me. I opened the door and there she was. *Carmil,* she says. *Carmil.*

We laughed. She's good at doing children, the face and hands and all. You can tell by the way Carmel imitates kids that she loves them.

—*Carmil.* Will yeh do us a favour, *Carmil?* I'll do one for you back, *Carmil.* I needed Tampax because I'd forgot to get them when I was going past the chemist so I said okay I'd do her a favour.

—She's making it up.

—How come I remember it then, Missis?

—You're making it up.

—I remember it, clear as day. I thought you wanted a lend of one of me blouses or something.

She turned back to Denise.

—Then she told me what she wanted me to do and I told her to fuck off.

—You did not. You'd never have said that in the house.

—I told you to fuck off.

—She didn't. You remember, Denise. Language in the house; we'd have been killed.

—Denise; look at me. I told Paula to fuck off.

I let her go on.

—So, of course, she put her Paula puss on her. You said you'd do it, *Carmil.* You said you'd do it, *Carmil.* So I gave in. I had to. Up the stairs, into the bedroom, the bleedin' toilet, down the stairs. She wouldn't get off my fuckin' back. You said you'd do it, *Carmil*. You said you'd do it, *Carmil*. So —

She lit her fag. Her timing is always brilliant. She'd have made a great doctor, Carmel would. You've got— a cold; just when the poor patient was convinced that she had cancer.

She put her wasted match back into the box.

—So, she said. —I went out. Down to Kearns. Houseful of brothers. Fuckin' mortified, I was. I knocked on the door. Mister Kearns answered.

—Now there was a ride, I said.

—Mister Kearns! said Denise.

—Yeah.

—The father!

—Yep.

—Jesus.

—He was fuckin' lovely, said Carmel. —Better-looking than any of his sons and everyone of them was a ride as well.

—He must have been ancient, said Denise.

—Younger than we are now, said Carmel.

That shut us up for a bit.

Then Carmel got back to the story.

—Anyway, Mister Kearns, the man himself, opened the door. I nearly died. —Yes? he says. —Is — ? I couldn't remember his name. I'm red as a fuckin' beet-root. Just standing there. With my mouth open. Cursing you, Paula. He's looking down at me. I'm standing there wanting to fuckin' die. Cos I was too lazy to go to the chemists myself. Jesus. He's staring at me, you know. —Is your son in? I said. —Which one? he says back. —I've seven of them. Jesus Christ; he's looking at me. —There's only four of them in if that's any good to you. He was being smart-arsed but he wasn't good at it; it made him seem dirty or something, d'you know what I mean, taking advantage of me or something. Cos I really fancied him, Mister Kearns. I thought he was fuckin' gorgeous. I used to mess with myself thinking about him.

—Carmel!

—*Carmil*. I did. I could come in thirty seconds, no problem, thinking about him. Then he went and ruined it by being smart-arsed. His voice didn't fit the rest of him either. It wasn't a very good-looking voice. Donald Duck, he sounded like. So I decided I wouldn't let him best me. —The one that's about thirteen, I said. —That'd be Martin, he said. —Yeah, I said. —Whatever. Will you give him a message? Will you tell him that Paula O'Leary wants to go with him. He's gawking at me now; he doesn't know what's happening. —Cos if you do that for me, I said, —she'll go to the shops and get me my jam-rags for me.

Jesus, the laughing.

—Don't mind her, I told Denise. —It never happened. And tell us anyway, I said to Carmel. —Who did you think about after that?

—What?

—When you were playing with yourself.

—Oh. Eddie Kearns. A minute and a half with him.

—When we were in the room?

—Yeah.

—Jesus, said Denise. —I never knew that.

She can sound very stupid sometimes; you'd feel sorry for her.

—I'll tell you another thing you never knew, said Carmel. —I did it with Derek Kearns.

Carmel asked him for me; as simple as that. She was

thirteen. I asked her would she and she did, after the usual no no no okay. She went up to him in the usual way. She was the same age as him. She went straight up. He was playing football. She went up to him after the game when he was picking up his jumper that was one of the goal posts. It was a green jumper, home-made looking, V-necked. They were all going home for their teas, all the other boys. We'd waited ages for the game to end. It went on all afternoon. On the big green behind our houses. It wasn't even a proper game; they just kicked the ball around and now and again tackled each other. Towards the end they hardly moved; they just tapped the ball to one another and waited till it rolled towards them. Carmel complained a bit but she stayed with me. All the fellas knew what we were doing there, that we were going to ask one of them to go with one of us. But they didn't know which one of us or which one of them. We enjoyed it; we had them anxious and excited. Excited about which one of them was going to be asked. Excited that it was going to be Carmel, worried that it was going to be me. I remember that. I remember it well because it didn't dawn on me until Carmel was going over to him. And it was too late to stop her. She said something to him and he nodded. He nodded. She was coming back. Carmel was lovely-looking in her own way. There'd been a thing written about her on a pole outside our house. It was done with chalk so it was easy to get off before our mammy or daddy saw it. He'd have blamed her for it. He was like that; he wanted to protect us. Carmel cried when she was cleaning it. Carmel O'Leary Has Big Tits. No spelling mistakes.

—He said yeah.

I went with him for three and a half weeks. Then I

81

broke it off because he was going to break it off with me and I wanted to get there first. No fella had ever broken it off with me. I kept thinking that he was only going with me because I was Carmel's sister. Dee and Fiona were green about it. I broke it off with him. Then I told them and they were even greener.

It was great then, that year or two, from ten to twelve or so. It was all fun. But it got complicated after that, and nasty.

Carmel's different. She remembers nothing good. She won't. That's just the way she is. Everybody remembers their First Holy Communion, or things about it. Not Carmel.

—Nothing, she says.

—Your dress.

—No.

—The money.

She shakes her head. She won't remember it for you. It's in there somewhere, in her head. She just won't let it out. She has her own version of things.

Her first kiss.

—A tongue that had hair on it; I'm not fuckin' joking yis.

Her first day at school.

—She hit me. Before I even sat down.

Her wedding day.

—Boring.

Our father.

—There's things you never knew about.

I heard Denise gasp when Carmel said that.

—What d'you mean? I said.

We were in Denise's kitchen. We had a bottle open and a carton of orange juice. The chipper papers were in a heap on the table. It was very unlike Denise to have left them there. She usually gets even tidier when she's drunk. I've seen her rearranging chairs and tables in the pub when she's pissed enough. I once even saw her using her sleeve to mop up a spill.

Carmel poured juice into her glass.

—What d'you fuckin' mean, Carmel?

Her hints; she'd been making them for years. I didn't want any more of them. They were getting in my way. She made them up as she went along.

—What're you saying?

—I'm saying nothing, she said.

—Nothing, I said. —You already said something. You started, so finish.

Denise had started clearing up the mess; hoping we'd go. I wasn't going anywhere.

—Sit down, I said to Denise.

She kept tidying up, avoiding us.

—What? I said to Carmel.

She stared at her glass. She opened her cigarette packet and rooted for one. I had to push Denise's arm out of the way; she was leaning over for my chip bag.

—What. Are. The. Things. That we don't know?

Denise shook a bag.

—There's some left.

—Fuck off, Denise, I said.

I looked at Carmel.

—Well? Hey; well?

She was crying.

It was the drink. You made things up when you were drinking and you believed them if you were drunk enough. They became absolutely true and real. I knew. Jesus, the things I knew for a fact when I was footless. Once — Jesus Christ — I knew Jack was dead. I was sitting on the top step of the stairs. I'd got him out of his cot and he was in my arms. I was crying. Squeezing him. The middle of the night. He was smiling up at me, then crying, but I didn't believe it. It was his angel. He was dead. He'd died while I was out. I knew it. Cot death. I'd have killed him to prove it. Charlo took him off me and brought him back to the cot, stopped him from crying. I sat on the step. I was grieving. Big lumps of grief climbed up through me. I enjoyed it. The strength of it. My love being proved.

—Fuckin' eejit.

Charlo stood above me at the bedroom door.

—It's my fault!

—Come on to bed, for fuck sake.

I hated him for that. He'd ruined it. I couldn't believe it any more and the grief became just snot and bits of prawn cracker. I'd never drink again. I swore it. Never again. I'd never leave the kids alone. I'd never drink again. I was hopeless. I was useless. But now I knew and it would be different from now on. No more. I went into Jack and John Paul's room. I looked down at Jack. I put my hand on his back to feel him breathing. All that strong breath, so quick; it was like he was growing, I could feel it. I didn't deserve him. I didn't deserve him. I was starting it again, nearly wishing him dead. To prove how hopeless I was, what a slut and an alco. On the front page of the Herald. Found dead while she was out drinking. That was me. I kissed John Paul. I got into the bed beside him. He woke me up in the morning. He was trying to get over me. God love him, he was terrified. His mother in her Sunday clothes and shoes beside him in the bed. And sick on the pillow. I turned the pillow over and closed my eyes.

I knew what Carmel was up to. She'd had a hard time from our father when she was a teenager; they never really recovered from it — they were always at each other, at Christmases and christenings — and now she was giving herself a good reason for hating him, making it up and believing it. Loving herself for hating herself. I knew well what she was up to.

My father never did anything to her.

17

It must have been him. On the ground, under a blanket. First the camera was far off; all you noticed was the car and houses behind it. There was the yellow accident tape warning people not to go near it and there were Guards inside the tape. One of them stepped over the tape; he was walking away from the camera.

I can remember nothing about what the reporter said, except two words.

—One man —

It was the reporter with the Northern accent. He looks nice, like he'd be happier doing something else for a living. I can't think of his name. The only one I can ever remember is Charlie Bird and it wasn't him.

—One man —

Then the camera homed in on the car, only it wasn't the car it was aiming at; it was Charlo beside it, in front of it, with the blanket over him, or it might have been something else, but he was covered. He must have been face down because his foot was hanging from the open door, the back of his foot and leg and it disappeared under the cover just before the knee. He must have fallen out of the car. It looked like he'd tripped up getting out. I didn't know the car. I knew the socks. Green diamonds. I'd bought them for him. The car was neatly parked; he'd fallen out onto the path. The houses looked nice — big with lots of trees. He was far from home.

18

My name is Paula Spencer. I am thirty-nine years old. It was my birthday last week. I am a widow. I was married for eighteen years. My name was O'Leary before I got married. My husband died last year, almost exactly a year ago. He was shot by the Guards. He left me a year before that. I threw him out. His name was Charles Spencer; everybody called him Charlo. Except his mother and my father. And the priest at his funeral. I have four children. (There could have been five; I lost a baby.) The oldest is Nicola. She is eighteen. She has a job in a shop and a steady boyfriend, Tony. She's a great kid. I don't have to worry about her. Next is John Paul. He is sixteen. I don't know where he is. He was squatting in some flats in town but I don't think he's there now. He never comes near me. Nobody talks to me about him. I never mention him to anyone. I have reason to believe that he's a drug addict. He has robbed my mother more than once. A druggie. He never comes here; he knows there's nothing. Heroin. He has a tattoo on his arm that I bought him; it's the only thing left between us. I don't mean that; it's how I cope. It's either that or pretending that everything is grand and he's still at home with me or on his way back.

I gave him the money for the tattoo on his fourteenth birthday, to stop him from hating me. Liverpool F.C. He doesn't even care about them any more. It's cruel; I don't know what happened. I'm always expecting another knock on the door, the news about John Paul. Every knock, every footstep outside kills me. Next is Leanne. She is twelve. She's lovely, wonderful; I'd love her to never grow up. I found a love-bite on her neck last Saturday. She saw me looking at her. I said nothing. She's hilarious. She always cheers me up. She's good in school but a bit cheeky, her teacher tells me. She's intelligent and creative and good at maths but too fond of smart remarks. She could spend more time at her homework. The teacher says. I'm going to make her stay in school until she's finished, right up to the Leaving Cert. The first of the Spencers to do it. Last is Jack, my baby. He is five. He's as bright as a button, and quick. He's a gentle little lad. He still has his baby's face and tummy. Whenever I feel really poor I always search for Jack and look at him; he looks well-fed and prosperous. Getting hugged by Jack is like nothing else in this world. I've taught him to sing Bye Bye Blues, and he knows when to sing it. I have spent more money on his clothes than on all the others put together. I've gone without food to make him look good. No hand-me-downs for Jack; no way. He is my mascot; my statement. He's my baby. He doesn't remember his father; he tells me he doesn't. (I'll never forget the time I saw a woman in the supermarket looking at Leanne. It was years ago. Something about it scared me. Her basket was empty. The woman saw me looking at her. —I recognise the coat, she said. She tried to smile and walked away. —Goodbye. I'd got the coat from the Vincent de Paul. Never again. The humiliation, Jesus, and there were other things that upset me then, and still do. Where was *her* daughter? It was the weekend. Why was her basket empty? It was just an ordinary blue coat. That poor woman.)

My father is dead. He died of cancer after a long fight. My mother is alive and well. She is sixty and lonely. I have two sisters and three brothers. I had another sister who died. I am close to my sisters but I don't see much of my brothers. I don't like Roger and he doesn't like me. I haven't seen him in years, not even at Christmas. He lives in England somewhere. My mother told me where but I didn't take it in; I don't care. He's divorced. Charlo once gave him a hiding. He had it coming to him.

I am an alcoholic. I've never admitted it to anyone. (No one would want to know.) I've never done anything about it; I've never tried to stop. I think I could if I really wanted to, if I was ready. I've always liked a drink, from when I was sixteen, even before I started going out with Charlo. I don't remember when I stopped liking it and started needing it. It crept up on me, I suppose. My father was never a big drinker and my mother doesn't drink at all.

(—Do you ever remember Daddy being drunk? I ask my sisters.

—No, says Carmel.

—Never, says Denise.)

Years ago, I had to drown the alcohol with coke or blackcurrant. Now I prefer orange juice, but I'll drink anything. I don't know when I started being like that. I don't know when I became an alco. My children have gone without good food because of my drinking. My children have suffered because of my drinking. But I have it under control. I've been taking back some of the day. I don't drink now until after Jack has gone to bed. I've been doing that for three months, a week and three days. It isn't easy. I stay out of the house; I bring him to the park. I put the bottles in the shed in the back and throw the key into the long grass around the edges of the back garden. I bought the lock and key especially for that, for locking away the bottle. The idea just came into my head. I threw out the spare key, threw it in the bin on bin day. I put a family-pack of crisps back on the supermarket shelf to make up the money for the lock. It's only a small one; I could prob-ably break it. But I won't. I'm proud of it. I search for the key after Jack's in bed. It can take ages but I always find it. In the rain and dark and the cold. I find it. But I don't mind once he's in bed. Sometimes I put him to bed a bit early. I don't enjoy it, the drinking. I don't remember when I did. I need it. I shake. My head goes; I have small blackouts. I start sweating patches of sweat. Yes! Yes! cries the girl, we all need a drink; that's a bit from a little book I used to read with Jack. I laughed and cried when I read it the first time. It gave me a fright; it seemed to be laughing at me. A little girl climbing up on a chair to get to the sink. A little girl with yellow hair, a green skirt and blue shoes. I used to drink all day. I had gin in my coffee in the mornings. Before Charlo died. Before I threw him out. He wasn't to blame for it. We always drank a lot together. It's only when you're alone that you begin to notice what you're doing. I went off the rails altogether when Charlo died. For a while; I don't remember. It's different now though. I'm coping with it, thinking about it. Deciding. I made Jack go to bed early last night. I put the kitchen clock forward so Leanne couldn't point out that it wasn't his bedtime — because she would — and I ended up having to send her up early as well. I remembered to put the clock back to its proper hour after she'd gone. A few months ago I wouldn't have remembered.

Progress.

I'd love to tell Nicola about it. She knows already; she's not stupid. She can see and smell. But I'd love to say it to her. I think I'd stop then. It would keep me on my toes, knowing that somebody knew what I was up to. Especially Nicola. Sometimes I forget she's my daughter, I want her to love me so much. It feels like the other way round; I'm the child. It's so reassuring just being in the same room as her. I calm down; I don't grab at the glass. I'd like to sleep in her bed sometimes but I never could.

I'd like to go to Alcoholics Anonymous but I don't have the time. I don't know if there's one local. I don't know how to find out; I can't ask. I can't ask the priest, the one that calls round every couple of months — every two months, drinking tea and eating cake with the deserted wives of the parish. Anyway, he stopped calling after Charlo got killed; I wasn't a deserted wife any more. And I wouldn't trust him as far as I'd throw him. The looks he gave me when he was talking about faith and the Blessed Virgin, it wasn't my tea he was after, or my biscuits. It isn't only the bishops who like to get their exercise.

Sometimes though, I'll take looks from any source. They remind me of myself; they wake me up. I'd go to bed with a priest if I fancied him enough; I think I would. But then again, I've never really seen a good-looking priest. Except for Richard Chamberlain in The Thorn Birds. I'm as well off with my hand and my imagination. Mind you, when you've seen what my hand does all day — wiping, scouring, cleaning other people's bins and toilets — my imagination has its work cut out.

I still think of Charlo.

I miss him.

I want him to come back.

Facts, Paula.

I get up at eight o'clock every morning. I used to sleep it out a lot; sometimes I couldn't get up. But not any more. I made the decision. I make the effort. I get up when the alarm goes. It's a little victory; I'm in charge of myself. I get up. I dress and wash before I go downstairs; I rub the cold out of myself. I shout in to the kids on my way down. I go in and tickle Jack. He has the boys' room to himself now. He looks so small in it. I make the breakfast. There's not much making in cornflakes but I do it, put the bowls on the table, spoons beside each bowl; I want to. I could never get any of them to eat porridge. My father believed in porridge. He believed it could do good things for you.

—Culchie food, said John Paul.

I wonder what he has for his breakfast these days.

Stop.

Leanne has tea. Jack has milk. I only got him to stop using the bottle last year. He'd started school; it was embarrassing. It took him ages to admit that it tastes just as nice out of a Winnie the Pooh mug. I did tests with him; it was like an ad. Now try Brand X.

—I want a bockle.

—It's a bottle.

—Yeah; I want it.

—Try this one.

—No.

—A little drop.

—No.

—A little sip just.

—No.

For fuck sake.

I have coffee, a two-spoon cup. Nicola has already gone to work when I get up. She's a pot-of-tea-before-I-say-boo-to-you woman. There's always a pile of warm teabags in the sink when I come down, like what a horse would leave behind.

So there's just me and Leanne and Jack in the mornings, except on Sundays when Nicola doesn't work. I like it. I like giving out to them, rushing them and pushing them. Come on, come on, chop chop. Making sure they have their lunches, checking they've all the right books in their bags. I'm on the case. It's a happy time. We're not poor first thing in the morning. They like it. They know I like it. I pretend I'm annoyed; they know I'm pretending. Sometimes I'm not and they know that too. Come on come on hurry hurry. Busy busy. Busy busy. They love it when I fly around the house saying that. Busy busy. Busy busy. Then they're gone. Leanne brings Jack. She brings him up to the door of the school and shoves him in. She waits to see that he's found his classroom, then she goes on to her own door around the corner. I followed them a few times, just to check. It was lovely. I followed them because there was supposed to be a child snatcher on the loose, a woman with stolen hospital records going up to houses and trying to take the children away. I heard it on the radio. It's big business, baby snatching, especially in America. It's a sick world.

I have half an hour or so to myself — another cup of coffee and a think — then I'm off. Four days a week I have cleaning jobs, houses. On top of the office cleaning later on in the day. I don't do anything on Tuesdays and I don't like them much. I should clean my own house, I suppose, but I couldn't be bothered. We usually clean the house together when there's so much dust that it has no room to settle. It's nearly a tradition now, a game. Leanne loves it. She wrote in a story for school that one of her hobbies was cleaning. God knows what the teacher thought when she read it. I sit around on Tuesdays, listen to Gaybo — Gerry Ryan's too much of a smart-arse for me. Sometimes I go down to Carmel for a chat, before I go to pick up Jack. Carmel's not too bad in the mornings; she only puts her fangs in after dark. I like the morning cleaning. Don't ask me why. I'm doing something useful. I'm getting exercise. I'm getting paid. I like seeing into other people's houses. Funny, I hardly ever feel jealous. And I should, because some of the houses are incredible. Huge. Some of the stuff in them, I wouldn't want most of it myself but it must cost a fortune. Dark furniture, flat-screened tellies, CD players with tiny little speakers. I love music. There's one house I do on Mondays, in Clontarf; they've a great collection of CDs, all the seventies stuff. I got her to show me how to use the CD player. There was no problem. I like her, the owner. Miriam. We're the same age. We both went to the same dances when we were kids. I don't remember her. She married a doctor. I married Charlo. Mott The Hoople, Bad Company, Sparks, Queen — they have them all. I might get a tape recorder and tape some of their stuff. I love the CDs. They're very stylish; I love the colours. They look expensive. I love the way you just a press a button and get the exact song. I don't know how many records I scratched and ruined when I was pissed.

—She's as sweet as Tupelo honey —

Charlo sang that to me, down on his knees.

—She's an angel of the first degree —

He'd just stood on a bee. We heard the crunch and started laughing; on the playground tarmac. I can't remember when; I don't think we'd been going together that long.

—I thought he'd get away, said Charlo.

—It might have been the queen, I said.

—Dead now anyway, said Charlo. — God love it.

—She's as sweet as Tupelo honey —

I love Van Morrison.

—Just like honey baby from the bee —

I love the music. They have speakers all over the house and no children; the house hardly needs cleaning at all. The music fills the time.

—You can take all the tea in China —

Put it in a big brown bag for me —

My cloth swoops over the sideboard. The brush swings around the toilet bowl. Van's my man. A walkman would be nice, for the other houses and offices in the evenings. I've seen cheap ones. And the train on the way home; it would be nice to close my eyes and listen and drift.

—You can take all the tea in China —

Things come back when I listen. The music drags out memories. That's one thing about my life; it has a great soundtrack.

Wooden floors are in; people don't seem to like carpets any more. Bare floors; pretending they're poor. I don't like it. I'd like to come home to carpet, get the shoes off, let the feet sink in; lie on it, lie back and float.

—Sail right around — round the seven oceans —

Clontarf, Sutton, Killester and Raheny; they're the

houses I clean. Raheny is the worst. You're only in the gate, you haven't looked up at the house yet, and you know: kids. The kids make shite of the house all week and I arrive on Fridays and clean it up so they can start all over again on Saturday. I think kids should clean up their own messes. Mine always did. Even Jack, even if he's actually making a bigger mess when he's doing it. It's unbelievable. Marker and paint on the walls and fridge, dirty clothes on the stairs, crumbs and bits of stood-on sandwiches all over the place. They mustn't do a stroke during the week. They wait for me. I even have to put the videos and CDs back into their boxes because the room would look untouched if I didn't. She doesn't work; she leaves the house when I arrive. She kind of sneaks; she looks guilty. So she should, the bitch. She gets home just when I'm leaving. I saw her sitting in her car once, outside their gate on the road, waiting for me to finish; I saw her from their bedroom window. Waiting for me. She's left me short a few times. —I'll see you next week. I forgot to get to the bank. It's not fair; I have to remind her the next week. I *need* that fuckin' money. It's Friday. She has no fuckin' idea. It's the only house I feel jealous in; the kids have everything. I know; I pick it up.

I come home past the school every day so I can pick up Jack. I'm often early but I don't mind. There are others there waiting; nothing else to do, some of them. I like a chat while I'm waiting. For a while after Charlo died I couldn't stand still in the one place; they were all looking at me and away from me — I saw it. I made sure I never had to wait; I got there right on time or a bit late. The teacher didn't mind. She probably felt sorry for Jack, him with no daddy and a smell of drink off his mammy. I'm better now though. I don't get restless. People have got used to me, the woman whose husband was shot. Once the kids come out the door the chatting stops; it doesn't continue after we've claimed our kids. We all walk home on our own. There are a few fathers there as well. They don't talk, not even to one another. They're embarrassed. No jobs to go to. Women's work. You'd feel sorry for them. They're great with their children, gently pulling and turning them so they can get their coats on, holding their hands, hugging them. Charlo was never like that. He wasn't a bad father in some ways — especially when the kids were small. He was great at inventing games and rolling around on the floor. Flinging them up and catching them. Letting them drench him with water. Unless he had his good clothes on him. But he'd never have pushed a pram or a buggy. Unless I was with him; never by himself. And he never dressed them. He never taught them anything. Even tying their laces; I had to teach them. He never looked at their homework. I wondered was he illiterate, if he'd been fooling me for years. But he just wasn't interested. He'd never have collected the kids from school. It's only up the road. They know the way. I'm busy.

Facts, Paula.

There's one of the men I talk to. I feel sorry for him; I'm not sure why. He's nice. You never know. He might be on his own. He collects a little girl. I asked Jack was she in his class. He said she wasn't but that doesn't mean anything.

—Are you sure?

—Don't know.

That's Jack.

I think he's younger than me, the man. (When do fellas become men? I never noticed.) He sometimes says hello first. He probably has a wife who works. He wears good shoes, strong black ones. He might work nights. (I have to admit it, I have a bit of a crush on him — like the crush I had on Mickey Dolenz from The Monkees. I wonder where that word came from. I've looked it up in Leanne's dictionary. It just says Infatuation. I had pictures of Mickey Dolenz in all my schoolbooks and all over my part of the bedroom wall. I loved him. I cried in front of the telly when he came on. Saturday night. We all watched it. Daddy said it was rubbish and he lost his temper when we started screaming. But I'm sure he was messing. He never stopped us from watching it. He called us a gang of scrubbers. But he was messing. I was seriously into Mickey Dolenz, as Leanne would say. Holding hands, that was all, walking down a beach while he sang Take A Giant Step all around us. I'd run and he'd run after me; I'd let him catch me and it would be his turn and he'd run ahead and keep looking back at me trying to catch up with him and he'd laugh and that would slow him; we'd end up in the water and it would be lovely and warm, like bath water.

—And take a giant step outside your mind —

But he wouldn't have an erection, the water wouldn't make my nipples stick out — nothing like that. We'd keep walking, the sun would go down, we'd share a bag of chips. He'd leave me home to my caravan. His would be two doors down from mine.

—Good night, Paula.

—Good night, Mickey.

He'd stop at the corner of the caravan and turn and grin and wave at me, and wink. I'd see him again in the morning. We'd do the exact same thing, start at one end of the beach and walk home. I never figured out how we got to the far end first. I didn't like Mike Nesmith. He was too old-looking; he'd have wanted his feel. Peter Tork was stupid. Davey Jones was a bit too small; men had to be taller than girls. I had a crush on Blue Boy too, from The High Chaparral. I'd go horse riding with him and it would be like flying; I wouldn't feel the horse under me. Robert Kennedy — I used to watch out for him on the News. I walked on the beach with him. He never took his suit off. He explained things to me. Funny, I wasn't that upset when he got shot; it didn't seem to matter. I kept walking with him until I left him for someone else. My mammy cried watching the News. I made up in my head that he was her cousin.

And I've had a few since I got married. Crushes. Stupid things. Nothing. No sex or adultery. Just things to fill the days really, although that wasn't what I felt at the time. There was a bus conductor I loved. I used to wait for his bus; I'd let the others go by. I found reasons to go into town, to buy things that I could just as easily have got in the shopping centre or even the local shops. The money I wasted on fares; Jesus. I nearly went mad trying to see if my conductor was on the bus before I'd get on it. I must have looked like a right eejit, sticking my hand out, gawking up, trying to see if he was upstairs, putting my hand back in my pocket because it wasn't him. They must have talked about me in the depot. The mad one. I couldn't help it. He was thin. He had day-old beard years before Bob Geldof invented it. I used to lie in bed worrying about him, if I thought he was on the late shift. He was lovely. He just took the fares and said Thanks, no smart remarks, no posing, no barrelling down the stairs like he was Starsky or Hutch. I imagined him, with his children, all boys for some reason. Bringing them places, cleaning up in the kitchen, watching Coronation Street, making a cup of coffee for his wife, not tea. Coffee that you had to make, not instant. Bewley's coffee. He never said anything to me except Thanks. All I said was One and two halfs into town, please. It didn't matter. I used to drag the poor kids in and out of town, in the rain and cold, just so he could take my money off me. Then, one day, I wasn't thinking about him any more.

I fancied a barman as well for a while. I saw him on Sunday nights when Charlo took me out. I don't know what it was; he wasn't particularly good-looking. He was so cool under pressure. He glided behind the bar. Black hair. He could hold three empty glasses in each hand, holding them under the taps. He didn't sweat much. I used to imagine that there'd be a knock on the door — or a ring or a buzz if the bell was working — and it would be this barman, Eamon. I could never think of a good reason why he'd be there. It annoyed me because I had to get him into the house. He'd knocked on the wrong door.

—Come in for a cup of tea anyway.

It didn't work.

He was looking for Charlo.

—Come in and wait; he'll be back soon.

That was better but there was a problem with it. What did he want Charlo for? They couldn't be friends; that would have ruined it. Charlo had left his jacket in the pub and Eamon was bringing it round for him. But Charlo went to the pub every day, so why couldn't he just wait? Because he wanted to see me. In one version, he tells me — later — that he'd robbed the jacket so he could have an excuse to call.

He wasn't a barman. He'd turned into a plumber or an electrician, some job that gave me a good reason for letting him into the house — not a milkman or a postman — I was never a slut in these daydreams. I was always completely dressed when I opened the door.

Most of what we did was talk. We held hands after a while. He put his head on my shoulder. It got darker. I did all the talking; he listened. Sometimes we said nothing; we just sat in the dark. It was always warm. We never got hungry. I had it all worked out. I spent hours in the kitchen, when Jack was having his nap, or in front of the telly or on the bed, going through the whole story, the same story once a day for months, changing it a bit, trying to convince myself. The point of it was the two of us sitting there for ever in the hour before night in a warm room where you never had to get up to go to the toilet. The work went into getting us there, arranging it that I didn't have kids or a fucker for a husband and that a man maybe ten years younger than me would fall in love with me. In one version I met him at Charlo's funeral. I even looked out for him at the real funeral; I remembered it, that version, when I was walking out of the church.

I could make myself cry very easily. My eyelids would tingle and go spongy; I could feel my eyes getting red. I could stop it then but I often let the tears come. I made up dreams about sex as well. Anywhere, any time. Mad things came into my head — men, Charlo, bits of fruit, everything. Mad things. The smell of the kids' nappies, the feel of a school-bag, putting on my coat, opening a can, bending to pick up a sock — I'd be gasping. It took nothing. No plan or story or time of day. I'd store up the sexiness, keep it away; rub against a wall, then stop and wait, store it up. I was for the birds when I was like that; I didn't know who or where I was. I had to count the children, two girls, two boys. I sat the dinner in the sink instead of the oven. I locked myself out of the house on purpose. I went into town and forgot why. I had no control over it. I stored it up. It got higher and higher. Then, when I got Charlo, I let go; it poured out. I sucked him, I bit him. I pulled his hair; I made him mad. He loved it, he hated it. I was all over him. It was me. I fucked him, I fucked him. He had nothing to do with it. It was all me. I laughed. I hit him. I nearly died. When I was empty, soaking wet and lying on the bed or floor, when I could think again, I loved him. My Charlo.)

Jack and me have the house to ourselves for a while when we get home. He has his cup of tea, I have my coffee; we sit and chat. I let him decide, the kitchen or the living room. He inspects them and makes his mind up, I don't know how. He creases his face while he's thinking. It's beautiful.

—This way.

He leads me to the chair.

—Now, Mammy.

I sit first, then him. He sips his tea. From his Winnie the Pooh mug.

—Very tasty.

He tells me nothing about school. He won't. I don't mind. He makes things up.

—What did you do today, Jack?

—America.

—You went to America?

—Yeah.

—How did you get there?

—We went to there.

I love it. Another couple of years and it'll be lying.
It's lovely now though.

—What did you see?

—Sweets.

—Lovely.

—Lovely sweets.

—Did you eat any?

—No.

—Why not?

—They were only the hard ones.

—No soft ones?

—No.

He started crying. I had to bring him down to the
shops and get him some soft sweets. I read books with
him; I've started doing that. I saw it in an ad. I never
did it with the other kids; I never thought. I saw this
ad, a picture in a magazine, for central heating or coal.
A man and his son in a big armchair in front of the
fire. The man was pointing at something in a big book
on his knee. The kid was cuddled up and gleaming. I
wanted to do that. And now I do. I love Winnie The
Pooh. I get a bigger kick out of him than poor Jack
does. I think he's fuckin' hilarious. The world it's all set
in; it's wonderful. Christopher Robin is always giving
parties. It's well for him, the little prick; he doesn't have
to pay for them. So Christopher Robin gave a party for
two heroes. Pooh was a hero for saving Piglet's life and
Piglet was a hero for giving Owl a fine house. Everyone
had a lovely party and the blustery day turned out to
be not so bad after all. I know it off by heart now. So
does Jack. I put in mistakes and he spots them and
makes me start again. It thrills me, how quickly he
catches them — he misses nothing. I take out Piglet's

name and put in Jack's. He loves that. Sometimes, I'm very happy.

Sometimes I have to get out. I can't stand it. I can't sit. I have to get out of there. Yes yes cries the girl, we all need a drink. I hate it. I hate myself. I hate the dirt and the emptiness and the stuffing coming out of the furniture, and nothing in the fridge. I can still smell Charlo in the house. I can't cope. The urge. The bottle. I have to get out.

—Come on, Jack.

We go to the park. The Hundred Acre Wood. We look for Tigger and Roo. Bouncy bouncy bouncy bounce. It's a long walk there and a long walk back. It kills the time; it keeps me away from myself. The air does me good. The key stays in the grass. We share a packet of crisps or Hula Hoops if I've the money on me. He feeds me, takes each one out on his finger and puts it into my mouth. He likes salt and vinegar; I prefer the ordinary. We leave a few in the bag for the ducks. Jack never objects; he never changes his mind. He tries to make sure that the ducks share. Talk talk talk, he never shuts up. He walks around every tree. I love watching. It makes me feel desperate; I'm aching with love and I'm dying for a drink. I tell the time by the light and the traffic. I can tell when it's time to go home. I'm like an Indian. I'm a squaw. My brave was shot by the Gardai.

—Home, Jack.

—Minute.

—Home love; come on.

I have to be home in time for Leanne. I won't give her her own key. I want to be there. I want her to smell food when she's at the door. I want her to be glad she's home. I know she is; I want to keep it that way.

I can still smell Charlo. Especially in the pillows.

I can't afford new ones.

I don't want new ones.

Facts.

Leanne does her homework. First thing when she comes home, I make her do it. Unless the weather is really lovely, then I let her out and she does it after her tea. She does it in the kitchen, under my eye. I didn't do that with the other two, Nicola and John Paul. I never thought of it really; they did it during the ads. Nicola did it during the ads she didn't like. Not Leanne though. I have to be gone by teatime and I want to make sure that she has everything done before I go. I had a good chat with her teacher about it. I love looking over her shoulder. Her stories are only brilliant; they're fantastic. She knows I'm looking. They're very funny, full of cheek. The only thing Mammy doesn't burn is the coal.

—You're not showing your teacher that, I say. —No way.

But she knows I don't mean it. It's my way of saying I think she's great. She concentrates and smiles; I can hear her brain working. Everything's neat; straight margin, red biro, lovely writing dead on the line. I wonder where she got the brains from.

Maybe from me.

I have to be out of the house by half-four. I feed them first. I have to leave Leanne in charge until Nicola gets home at half-five. I don't mind it too much; I trust her — I have to — and she's great with Jack. She does the dishes for me.

I'm off. Into town to my little office job. Paula Spencer, queen of the Pledge and J-cloth. I go in on the DART. There's a gang of us; we take up half a carriage.

We make more noise than the kids coming home from school. They're a gas shower, some of them. I like Mona a lot; I'd nearly call her a friend. She was very good to me after Charlo. Mona's seen me drunk and covered in my own vomit and she still sits beside me. I'd know her better only her husband can't stand the sight of me; I can tell. Still, the trip into town with Mona and the rest, it's like a tonic; it's like a fuckin' good drink. I miss it at the weekends. There's Gwen and Fran as well. Fran's like me, a widow-woman. She's eight years younger than me, with five kids. She's always laughing but you can see what's behind it; you can see it in her face, her eyes go red, her mouth stretches. Her laugh comes out like a scream. She loved John, her fella; he fell in front of a train. He jumped. He fell. The train hit him bang on. I remember, before her husband fell onto the tracks, we were all going into town together. It was before Charlo died. I'd thrown him out. Fran always slagged Charlo, for the crack. She knew I liked it.

—Seen your Charlo again last night, Paula.

—Her ex-Charlo, said Mona.

—In the Chinese again, said Fran.

Gwen joined in.

—He scored a hat-trick on Sunday. Isn't that massive now?

—He bought a curry chips, said Fran. —And a spring roll as well.

—Oh, I love them, said Gwen. —They're lovely.

—No meat though, Paula, said Fran. —He won't score many more hat-tricks if he doesn't eat his meat.

I nearly cried I was so happy. I felt close and even wanted. Just for as long as the trip into town. What can I say now to poor Fran? He didn't jump; he fell. I look at her. She's miles away but she's still there in the seat in front of me. I can see her mind skidding back and forwards, here and gone, here and gone; valiumed up to her hairline. She looks as old as me now; she's passing me by. It gives me no pleasure.

Mona has one of her kids going to college. I haven't a clue what he's doing; some college up in Dundalk. He's there two years now. He comes home at the weekends with a bagful of washing. She hangs up his knickers like they're flags. I'm not being bitchy; I don't blame her. She never boasts about it.

Leanne and Jack will go to college, a real one in Dublin.

Now now, Paula.

And they'll do their own fuckin' washing.

I get off at Tara Street. The rest go on to Pearse Street.

—Go easy with the Pledge, Paula.

—Don't worry.

I don't mind the cleaning, except for the time of day. I should be at home, like everyone else. There's something inside me fighting. I like the idea of me working. It's not glamorous — Dolly Parton won't be playing me in the film — but it's my job. I do it; I earn money for my family. It's just the time of day. I'm knackered. And guilty — I should be at home. The building is so empty, except for the noise of other hoovers. It scares me a bit sometimes. I'd like to see the offices when they're being used and full of people and noise. They'd look completely different. It's not like cleaning a house. When you're doing a house there are places that you look forward to getting to, because of the way the sun comes through the window or because it's the kitchen and the kettle or because it's a kid's room. It's like travelling through a small country; every bit is different. It's like being a spy or reading a book.

The floor I clean — the offices — they're nice; some of the rooms hardly need cleaning at all, ever. But it's very, very, very boring. There's the odd photograph of children, and gonks stuck on top of the computer screens, and sometimes a pair of socks in a drawer — I have a root through the open drawers now and again — but that's all. You're pushing your hoover through square feet of carpet that have nothing to do with people — when you should be at home with your family, putting your feet up or going out or anything else. It isn't natural. It's a fight.

It's easy. But my back gets at me. I know I shouldn't bend over when I'm hoovering; there's no need for me to do it — any specks on the floor are more than willing to be sucked up. It's a habit, shoving the hoover through the floor; you're not doing it properly if your hands aren't numb. There aren't many real walls. It's open-plan, all partitions. I wouldn't be mad about it. I prefer a wall; you need something to lean against. It must be hard to concentrate when you're working, everybody screaming down the phone, charging around the place. It's an insurance company, something like that; it's hard to tell from the papers left on the desks and in the bins. The company name is no good, just three surnames; no hints there. It's strange really, not knowing who you're working for. There's me, a vital cog in the machine, and none of the other cogs have ever seen me. I don't really know any of the other women, the cleaners, except Marie. She's the boss, the supervisor — but she has to clean as well, the floor above me. She comes down to my floor for the break.

She has a caravan in Courtown, the same as my sister Denise, but they don't know each other.

—There's more caravans than people sure, Paula.

—You'd know her if you saw her.

—Yeah; probably.

That's typical of our conversations. Chats about nothing, round and round. The price of food, the weather, the telly; that's us. I watch Coronation Street now — I tape it — because Marie watches it and we can talk about it. We never go too far, say anything that might embarrass. I'd love to, I have to admit; I think Marie would listen. I'm an alco, did I tell you? My husband killed a woman, did I tell you? Then he got shot by the Gardai, did I tell you? I cry at night. I lock the bottles in the shed and throw away the key. It wouldn't be fair though. She has problems of her own; I'm sure she does. There are things she never mentions. She has five kids but she's never talked about the oldest one — never, not even a name — and the youngest is mentally retarded. We'll never get to know each other. We go our separate ways. I go home on the DART. She goes home on the bus; I don't know what number. She gives me my pay on Thursday.

—Don't spend it all in the one shop now, Paula.

—It'll be gone before I get to the shop.

Home.

I don't like walking back to Tara Street. Not just the dark, it's the emptiness; there's no one on the street at that time, along the river. It gives me the creeps. All the traffic comes from behind me. It's not a long walk but I hate it. It's better when I get to the station. There are other people, all like me, going home. Some of them with a few drinks in them after work; you can tell from their faces and the serious way they walk. Up the plastic tube to the platform. I stay near the escalator. I don't go too far down the platform. I sit and hum. I get ready for the rest of the evening. I get rid of the cleaning ache and the drink ache takes its place. Yes yes, says the girl. I get up when the light turns green. I like to watch the train coming into the station, sailing in, the lights on, quiet and smooth; I love it. I always get into the same carriage, the first one. The same seat; it's usually free at that time. Some of the same people. I lean into the window and watch. Over the river, past the Customs House, the Irish Life building — I can see myself in the glass; I'm looking well from that distance — over Talbot Street, into Connolly. I've fallen asleep once or twice. It's always the same; you wake up just when it's too late. The train's stopped, the doors are open, it's your stop. You get up, you stagger to the doors, the doors shut. Too late, a little jolt, the train crawls out of the station. Shit shit shit. People looking at you. Nudging one another. Shit shit. It's such a waste of time. You smile. Ha ha. I did it on purpose. Ha fuckin' ha; such a waste of time. The first few weeks I could hardly stay awake; tiredness and the train, they both had me sliding down onto the floor of the carriage. It's not so bad now. I'm a veteran. I'm a scrubber, first class. I've won medals. I read a magazine if I find one in an office bin. I never take them off the desks. I've found books in the bins a few times. I couldn't believe it the first time. A book! Thrown away. A big fat five-hundred-pager. Danielle Steele. It was shite, but I loved it. I've seven of them now in my bedroom, in alphabetical order. All saved from the bins. Catherine Cookson is my favourite. I've two of hers. She's very good. Both out of the same bin.

Home.

It's a ten-minute walk from the station. A safe walk. People know who I am; I know them. I know the paths and the bumps. I know what goes on. I don't care much. I'm not curious any more. I like it here. I went through a lot. They saw it all. I'm still here. People are gentle. They left me alone. They smiled; they went out of their way. They had a whip-round for me. You don't expect to have to pay for your husband's funeral; it's not one of the things you plan for when he's forty, especially when he hasn't lived with you for over a year. People were good to me. This is where I belong. I wouldn't move. A few palm trees would be nice though, and maybe a lake.

In the door; yippee. Home. Ten past eight. The telly's on. Leanne and Jack are in with Nicola. They've been fed. The kitchen's clean. I don't have to look. Sometimes Jack is in his jim-jams. He still wears a nappy for bed. I left it off for a few nights but he had his bed soaked by the time I was ready for bed; I'm not ready for the fact that he's a wetter, like Leanne and John Paul were; it's too tiring. Soon. Anyway, I love the shape the nappy gives him under the jim-jams. It makes him look cuter and two years younger. (I wet the bed myself. Just once. The shock; the fright. Jesus. The shame. The relief that Charlo was dead and not beside me. That was the blackest time, the five minutes after I felt the cold and recognised it. Realising that I could do that. That I'd done it. The temptation to just throw the sheets on the floor and get back under the dry blankets. My head throbbing, too dry for tears. Those dry sobs that always seem phoney. But I got up. I managed. I brought the sheets down to the machine — at four in the morning. I turned the mattress over. I flipped it over like it was toast. It hadn't soaked through.) I sink into the couch beside Leanne. Jack climbs up. Nicola's there; she's glad to see me. Half a smile. My children.

Three of my children.

Baywatch.

—There's something wrong with those women.

—There isn't, says Nicola.

—What? says Leanne.

—They're gorgeous, says Nicola.

—What's wrong with them? says Leanne.

—Nothing, says Nicola.

I just say it — or something like it — to get them going.

—Their shoulders, I say. —Look it.

—That's just from the swimming, says Nicola.

—What's wrong with them?

—They're enormous.

—That's only from the swimming.

—Steroids as well.

—No way.

—Must be; look at them, Nicola.

—They're only shoulders.

—They're like boxers' shoulders.

—It's the swimming.

—How do steroids work?

She gets annoyed, Nicola; she's very loyal to the things she likes. I stop.

—How do steroids work, Mammy?

—I don't know. Injections.

—I like injections, says Jack.

—Do you, love?

—Yeah.

—Did you have any injections today?

—Yeah.

111

—How many?

—Seven.

—Were they sore?

—No.

How many injections did John Paul have today?

Jesus.

It's too much.

The ads come on.

—It's over now, Jack. Bed.

—It's not over. It's the ads.

He's right. I want to kill him.

—Bed, I say. —Come on.

Nicola looks at me. She knows.

It's the rule: I don't drink till he's gone to bed. He's going to fuckin' bed. Loads of tears — another look from Nicola — but I don't care. I *do* care. I'm lying, I'm cheating. I'm mistreating Jack. I know, I know. But I'm doing it anyway. It's not a life or death thing, I'm only sending him to bed early, I need a fuckin' drink! It's not fair, it's not fair. It's been a long day, I've been very good. Now it's my turn. I won't drink till he's in bed so that's where I'm bringing him.

I don't cheat on that. I go up the stairs with him. He leads the way; we go at his pace.

—I'll read you a story, don't worry.

Not just because I feel guilty either; I read him a story every night. Every night. No matter how desperate I am, shaking, in pain — I won't be able to find the key, it'll be too dark — I read Jack a story. No short cuts; I read every page. Jack knows every word. He stops me whenever I'm wrong and makes me start the sentence again.

—The milkman's bottles were clunking —

—No; clinking.

—Clinking. That's right. — as he —

—You start again.

—The milkman's bottles were clinking as he —

I can hardly see the words. Sometimes. My eyes are glueing. I have to scream. My joints are stuck. I'm in agony. I'm made of sore cement. I want to hit him, he's so fuckin' vigilant. Waiting for mistakes; the story means nothing to him. He doesn't care about me.

But I finish. I always finish. I never cheat. I'm not let. I close the book.

—That's that, Jack.

—Another one.

—No, love; not tonight. I'm going to bed myself. I'm very tired.

—You've had a busy day?

—Yeah.

I kiss him. He kisses me.

—Night night, love.

—Night night.

I turn the light off.

—Leave the door open.

—Sure.

—Go.

—Okay; night night.

—Go now.

—Night night.

I go alright. I nearly fall down the stairs. I step out in front of me. I don't care how I get there. I can take any pain on top of what I have. Let me out; I'm suffocating. Down the stairs. Down the hall. Through the kitchen. Pull back the curtain. I need the light for my search. Unlock the door. One of my terrors: the key will break in the lock. Out. I know where to look. Out. I cheated today. I followed the key to check where it

113

landed. I knew I'd be like this. I've been good; I don't have to suffer. I could stop it if I wanted to. Anytime I want. The grass is wet. When I'm not so busy. I'm not wearing my shoes. I don't care. I won't die. I know where the key is. Just the light from the kitchen. Resting on top of the grass. It was this morning. Unless a bird got it. Or a dog or a hedgehog — I saw one once. I can't see it. I'm in the way of the light. It's not there. Some cunt of a rabbit's after running away with it. The key the key. I won't break the lock. I will. Calm down. I won't break the lock. I'm in control. No more vomiting, no more blackouts. I got rid of that. I'm on my knees. It was there this morning, exactly there; I counted the steps. It was here. I can go to the off-licence. No money no money. I could stop tonight. I'm pulling the grass. It's not here. Break the lock. I'll get a new one. Just this once. I'll start again. I'll pour the rest down the sink. I will. It's only a lock; it's not the law. Just this once. The key! I've got it! I'm in control. I'm crying, I'm shaking. I can't get the key in. Stop, calm down. You'll drop the bottle. I'm blocking the light. Done it. Open. The bottle the bottle. I close over the door. I can't be seen. Off with the top. Up to my mouth. Head back, down. I hate it I love it I hate it I love it I hate it I love it I love it I love it. I'm younger. I'm fit. I'm slim and warm.

No more pain.

Back into the kitchen.

My feet are freezing.

I hate it. I can think now. I'm loose. I'm warming up. I can give up. Anytime I want. I'm going to. I'll go into the girls now. No shaking. Into a glass. Glug glug. I'll always love that sound. There might be something on the telly, something worth watching; I'm not really fussed. I keep my orange juice hidden. I have to do it; they'd drink it if I didn't. A brand new carton up on top of the press, well back. Can't be seen. I've checked.

In to the girls.

Up to Jack first. I leave my glass in the hall. I don't need it now. I'm calm. Up to Jack. I love him so much. I want to see him. Fast asleep. His fists over the cover. His little face; his fringe. I can cry looking at him. Fast asleep. Wish I could sleep like that. In the Land of Noddy-nod.

Back for a refill, into the kitchen. I'm grand now. All relaxed; nice and lazy. A nice way to end the day. I deserve it.

In to the girls.

—Hiyis.

They know.

No, they don't.

I don't care.

Nicola might but not Leanne. I don't care. No one's perfect, I do my best. They've nothing to complain about. Don't know what they're watching. It doesn't matter. Music and people running. Kissing. More running. The usual shite. I'm not following it.

Back in for a refill. Hugging the wall. Take me to the kitchen. I'll fill it again while I'm here. Save myself a journey. Glug glug glug. The sound of music.

Jesus Jesus.

Where am — The kitchen.

Room for more if I make some.

God, I hate myself.

Alco. Alco. Paula the alco.

I'm smiling into the kitchen window. I always look good in the kitchen window. I know it's me. I close the curtains. I lean out and miss the curtain by a foot.

That's me finished. I can control what I'm doing. I know when to stop. I won't be making chips. I don't want to break anything.

Back to the telly. Refill first.

The wall. In.

I sit down. I won't speak.

My head's falling. Stop it.

The girls have gone. Ah well. Telly's off. I just fell asleep. It's been a long day. Night night, everybody. Night night. See you in the morrr-ningggg.

—When you wish upon a star —

Makes no difference who you are —

Anything your heart desires —

Will come to youuu —

19

Charlo and my father. High Noon. The two of them standing there, facing each other, staring, my father at the window, Charlo at the door. My mother trying to get out of her chair, trying to smile. Denise and Wendy on the floor looking at The Golden Shot. The rest were out or upstairs.

Sunday afternoon.

I'd brought him home for tea. I'd been told to.

—I want to see him, said my father.

—He's very nice, said Mammy.

—I want to see him anyway, he said. —It's about time I met him.

They looked at one another, Daddy and Charlo. I hadn't told Charlo to be nice; I was hoping he'd put on a bit of a show. He turned up in his usual gear, the parallels and bomber jacket. Wearing denims on a Sunday was a big thing back then; it was almost like saying that you didn't believe in God. And his bomber jacket, zipped up even though it was lovely out, real spring weather. I thought he looked great but I could see him now through my father's eyes. I saw him looking at Charlo's socks. Mammy was still trying to lift herself out of the chair. She wasn't fat or awkward or anything; she probably just felt weak. I know I did.

—This is Charles, I said.

I nearly burst out laughing.

—Charles, said my father.

—Howyeh, said Charlo. —Mister O'Leary.

He was trying. I really loved him now. He was doing it for me, wrecking his Sunday, doing his best.

—Howyeh, Missis O'Leary.

God, he was gorgeous.

—Hello again, Charles, said Mammy.

I don't know why she said that; *again*. Maybe she sensed that Daddy was going to like Charlo — she often guessed things wrong — and she wanted to remind him that she'd seen him first. Maybe she hoped it would help us relax. He was the first fella I'd ever brought home. I was eighteen.

Twenty-one years ago.

—Sit yourselves down, said Daddy.

—We're watching Bob Monkhouse, said Mammy. Charlo said nothing.

—D'you like Bob Monkhouse, Charles? said Daddy.

—He's alright, said Charlo.

—We like him.

—He's good guests, said Charlo.

I nearly fell off my chair. He was really trying.

117

—He does, said Daddy. —Sometimes.

Daddy looked at Charlo looking at the telly. He was being horrible; I remember. He was waiting. He was going to get Charlo — I could see it. He looked mean that afternoon. We watched Bernie The Bolt put the arrow thing in the crossbow. Wendy was scratching her leg, trying to keep up with Charlo, the telly and Daddy. Denise was just staring at Charlo.

—I wonder is it all a cod, said Daddy. —What d'you think, Charles?

—Don't know, said Charlo. —The prizes are real.

It was a brilliant answer; it shut Daddy up. It made me nervous though. It was more like the real Charlo, much more than cheeky.

—Left a bit, said Mammy, and she laughed.

—Mammy! said Denise.

—Catweezil's on after this, said Daddy. —Although, God knows, the reception could be better. D'you like Catweezil, Charles?

—No, said Charlo.

I'll never forget how uncomfortable the chair was that afternoon. I can still feel it.

—Do you not?

—I think it's stupid, said Charlo.

—We like it, said Daddy.

—It's a kid's programme, said Charlo.

—We like it.

—It's brutal.

—We like it.

There was nothing after that.

The contestant in The Golden Shot won a car but no one said anything.

Tea, a few laughs, the two of them going off together for a pint, me and Mammy staying behind pleased with ourselves — there was never a hope. Did I think I was going to be able to write through this without hitting the fact that my father had decided to hate Charlo before he even saw him? Charlo was dead right, letting him know that he didn't give a fuck what he thought of him. If it hadn't been Charlo — if it had been a lad in a suit with a car and aftershave and a good job with a pension it would still have been the same. I knew that the whole thing was going to be a disaster. My father was a nice man but he could be very contrary and stubborn. He was being protective, I suppose; no one was good enough for his daughter. He *was* a nice man. But something was always going to happen that afternoon. I'd known all along, but they had to meet eventually. It was me and Charlo now. Charlo's clothes, my hair, Carmel's skirt — something would be said and bang! Some excuse, any excuse. But not Catweezil. I hadn't anticipated that. The whole thing ruined by fuckin' Catweezil.

Mammy got up to go to the kitchen. I was going with her. I'd given up. It was my father's fault; I have to say that.

—Catweezil's on now, he said.

—I'll be back in a minute, she said.

—You'll miss the start.

—There's the ads first; I won't miss much.

—Don't ask me what happened while you were gone, he said. —That's all I'm saying.

I remember every moment and detail. I remember it better than this morning. I followed Mammy into the kitchen. I didn't care about leaving Charlo with Daddy. There was no point. They hated each other; they were always going to. I didn't blame Charlo. It was my father.

Mammy pretended. I let her. I pretended too; it was

119

a nice occasion, the ham was nice and thick, the rain was staying away. I made sure that the butter wasn't too hard. I wiped the salad-cream and ketchup bottles. Daddy hated them dirty. I scraped the hard ketchup off the lid with a knife. I put the cat's tray out on the back step. That was where it went when we were eating. I wondered what was happening in the living room. Nothing; they'd both be staring at the telly, hating each other's guts. I didn't care.

I was seething, becoming furious.

I sliced the bread. Mammy put the lettuce, the tomato, the egg, the scallions, the ham on each plate. I looked at Mammy. It was strange, and still is even though I've gone through the same amount of years now myself: she was different. She wasn't the same person she'd been when I was smaller. She used to be bigger, happier, noisier. Lots of things were different. It wasn't just that she was older. She was still young; she was probably younger than I am — she was only eighteen when they got married. She was grinning away and concentrating and blocking out everything except the salads on the plates — and she looked miserable. She looked so sad. She hadn't worn a new piece of clothes in years. She didn't drink, she didn't smoke; she didn't do anything except sit in front of the telly and watch the programmes that he put on and say yes and no when he spoke to her: she didn't even knit.

It wasn't just her. He was different too. He'd become a bitter little pill and a bully. He made rules now just to make us obey them, just to catch us out. He used to laugh a lot but now he couldn't or wouldn't and he hated hearing laughter in the house. That was why he liked Catweezil, because it wasn't fuckin' funny. Charlo was right; it was brutal.

He used to be different. I know he was; I remember it. He used to play with us and act the eejit, always saying and making up stupid things.

—Be the hokey mokey mac.

He said that to get on our nerves, out loud so the whole street could hear him. He liked pretending he was from the country. Or he'd put on an English accent.

—Stop saying it's good for the garden, George.

He said that every time it was raining. It was from an ad. He said it for years.

Then he stopped. And Charlo in the house was making me notice it.

—A little warmer, said Mammy, —and we could nearly have it in the garden.

—Yeah, I said. —It's lovely.

—Are the bottles nice and clean?

—Yeah.

Charlo was right. It was pointless trying to please him; he'd never do it. Mind you, I didn't fully realise then that Charlo wouldn't have crossed the road to please anyone. Him and my father were very alike. She said — twenty-one years later. The wise old woman of the bottle.

20

A post mortem by the State pathologist found that Mrs Fleming had been struck twice across the face but there was no evidence of a sexual assault.

121

That was the part that made me get sick as I read it. Not the killing, the murder. I was ready for that.

. . . there was no evidence of a sexual assault.

My stomach fell, and hot sour liquid rose up. I managed to get my head to the side and my hair out of the way and I vomited onto the kitchen floor. I nearly followed it. Carmel held me.

. . . there was no evidence . . .

Jesus Christ. The hugeness of it; the evil. There were things that had happened in that house that I'd never know about. Because there was no evidence. There were no witnesses. No one and nothing.

—It's okay, love, said Carmel.

The things we say. Sometimes they make no sense, sometimes they're just packed with lies. I'm grand. Don't mind me. *You fell*. It's okay, love.

—What did he do, Carmel? I asked.

She just held me.

From the beginning.

My husband, Charles 'Charlo' Spencer, murdered a woman. Mrs Fleming. Gwen. A fifty-four-year-old housewife. The wife of Mr Kevin Fleming, a fifty-three-year-old bank manager. The mother of three grown-up children. He killed her with a shotgun. In her kitchen.

Back further.

Mrs Fleming answered a ring or a knock on her door, probably both, on Thursday morning, the seventeenth of February, 1994. It was before eight o'clock. She opened the door and my husband and another man, Richard 'Richie' Massey, were there waiting for her. They were wearing balaclavas; runners, blue jeans and black zip-up jackets. One of the men was holding a shotgun — *brandishing* a shotgun, it said in the Herald. That was my husband. The other man, Richard 'Richie' Massey, pushed Mrs Fleming back into her hall. She fell back and screamed. The two men followed her in and closed the door. The man with the shotgun ran to the kitchen — he knew exactly where he was going — and met Mr Fleming as he was coming from the kitchen to see why his wife had screamed. He was dressed for work but had not put on his shoes. This was what my husband said to Mr Fleming:

—Good morning, good morning, good morning.

Mr Fleming asked him what he wanted and tried to see past him, to see that his wife was alright.

—She's grand, said my husband.

Mr Fleming saw Mrs Fleming standing up. He called her name. Richard 'Richie' Massey grabbed Mrs Fleming's arm and pulled her towards the kitchen. Mr Fleming saw his wife looking at the phone on its table as she went past it. He thought she looked very calm, that perhaps she was in shock. She said nothing. She didn't resist. She just looked at the phone.

—Into the kitchen, please, Kevin, said my husband.

He jabbed Mr Fleming with the barrel of the shotgun. Mr Fleming was shocked at how painful it was; he actually thought he'd been shot. For a second. Then he did what he'd been told to do. The other man, with Mrs Fleming, followed my husband and Mr Fleming into the kitchen.

—Very nice, said my husband. —Even nicer when you're inside.

Mr Fleming remembered his exact words. Mr Fleming knew then why the men were in his house.

—Right, Kevin, said my husband. —Here's what's what.

Mr Fleming remembered the exact words.

—You'll go to work. To the bank. You'll get twenty-five thousand pounds in tens and twenties. You'll put them in a bag. You'll give it to my pal, my associate here. How's that sound?

My husband then turned to Mrs Fleming.

—Stick the kettle on, Gwen, he said. —Like a good girl.

Mr Fleming remembered. Emer O'Kelly started reading the news headlines. It was eight o'clock. Alan Dukes alleged that there was a whispering campaign against him in Fine Gael; the ANC had given major concessions to the Zulu-based Inkatha Freedom Party; Sir Patrick Mayhew said that the end of violence could transform the North's economy.

—I'll tell you one thing, said my husband. —It's cold out there. You'd want your coat.

He was taller than Mr Fleming. He bent down a bit and looked into Mr Fleming's eyes.

—Your grey one.

Mr Fleming saw the face grinning through the balaclava. Richard 'Richie' Massey laughed.

—What do they want, Kevin? said Mrs Fleming.

—A cup of tea, Gwen, said my husband. —Any questions, Kevin?

Richard 'Richie' Massey was going to accompany Mr Fleming. My husband was going to stay with Mrs Fleming. Richard 'Richie' Massey was going to phone the Fleming home when he had the money in his possession. My husband would then leave.

—No questions asked, said my husband. —You'll need your shoes.

Mr Fleming's shoes were in the kitchen. He had polished them the night before and left them on a sheet of newspaper. Mr Fleming sat down and put on the shoes. He was surprised that his hands weren't shaking as he knotted the laces; he was quite pleased about this. He tried to comfort Mrs Fleming. He assured her that she wouldn't be harmed, that it would all be over in no time. My husband agreed with him. Mr Fleming felt that his wife didn't really know what was happening; she was in a daze. He wondered if she had been hit when she'd fallen in the hall, or before. There was no reddening, or any other marks on her face. He remembered later that he was glad that she was dazed; the ordeal was easier for her that way.

My husband sat at the kitchen table. He rested the shotgun barrel on the back of the chair beside him, aimed at Mr Fleming.

—The kettle, Gwen, he said.

When Mr Fleming had laced his second shoe he went to the kettle and lifted it to check that there was enough water in it. My husband did not object. Mr Fleming switched on the kettle.

—Pity now you can't stay for a chat, said Charlo. —Duty calls but.

Mr Fleming remembered his exact words.

Richard 'Richie' Massey held Mr Fleming's arm. It was a mean grip, unnecessary. Mr Fleming resisted it long enough to stop and kiss his wife's cheek. Again, he assured his wife that everything would be alright.

—What's going to happen, Kevin? said Mrs Fleming.

—Nothing, love, Mr Fleming remembered saying. — I'll be back home in no time; nothing.

—Don't worry, Kevin, said my husband. —We won't get up to anything while you're gone. That right, Gwen?

Mr Fleming remembered that that was when he first felt really terrified. He didn't want to go. He was scared, not of anything that was going to happen to him but of what he was leaving behind.

—Let her come with me, he said to my husband.

—Ah now, Kevin, said Charlo. —Don't be stupid. It'll be alright; don't worry.

He pointed the shotgun at Mrs Fleming.

—Off you go, he said to Mr Fleming.

Richard 'Richie' Massey brought Mr Fleming into the hall and out to his car. (I'd never heard of Richard 'Richie' Massey. I resented it. Even when I thought I was going to vomit again. It upset me that Charlo had done all this with someone I'd never known.)

Mr Fleming drove.

That's where the facts about Charlo stop, until the last big one.

Mr Fleming drove his own car, a Volvo. There was no other car in his drive, and none that he noticed on the road outside his house. Richard 'Richie' Massey sat in the passenger seat and turned on the radio. He stuck his finger in the cassette socket.

—Any good tapes? he said.

Mr Fleming indicated the cassette rack between the seats and Richard 'Richie' Massey spent the rest of the short journey flicking through the cassettes. He rarely looked up.

—Load of shite, he said, more than once.

He didn't notice the roadblock.

The Flemings lived in an estate between Malahide and Portmarnock. Mr Fleming drove his car onto the Coast Road, turned left and headed for Malahide. He looked in the rear-view mirror. There was one car behind him, none in front. The traffic was usually heavier. He remembered thinking that and wondering if it meant anything.

Richard 'Richie' Massey didn't have a gun of his own. They must have — him and Charlo — they must have decided that the only thing they needed to control Mr Fleming was Mr Fleming's love for his wife; he wouldn't do anything to put her in more danger. (From what I've read, they were right: Mr Fleming loved Mrs Fleming.) Either that or they just couldn't get another gun in time and they decided to go ahead with the plan anyway; I don't know.

The roadblock was on the Coast Road, just before Oscar Taylor's restaurant. Mr Fleming saw it ahead. It spanned both sides of the road. It wasn't the more usual check-point; they weren't looking for tax and insurance. It was definitely a roadblock. For him. He looked at Richard 'Richie' Massey. He was still flicking through the tapes. Mr Fleming didn't slow down.

—All classical shite, said Richard 'Richie' Massey. — Have you no jazz?

Mr Fleming hoped that by coming at the roadblock at speed the Gardai would be alerted before he stopped. He was right. Armed men ran at the roadblock. A police car was put straddling the road behind the block; the driver got out and ran. Mr Fleming braked. The car skidded. Richard 'Richie' Massey was thrown forward and hurt. His face hit the dashboard. The car stayed on the road. Mr Fleming got out and ran to the roadblock.

—They have my wife! They have my wife!

He was surrounded by armed and unarmed Gardai,

uniform and plain-clothes; more Gardai went past him. He was dropped to the ground.

Mr Fleming couldn't see the man who spoke.

—She's in the car?

—No no. At home. At home. Please!

21

The wedding day. Patches of it were wonderful; nothing has changed that. I've good memories and some nice photographs. The ones taken outside the church. I look lovely. Charlo looks handsome. I look modern; you'd never think it was long, long ago. The flares on Charlo's trousers are the big give-away. And the hairstyles. All the hair split down the middle. People stood differently too back then, like they weren't confident, like their jackets were too small for them. Still though, it's not a bad-looking bunch of people. Both families. The aunts and uncles, cousins. Boyfriends and girlfriends, husbands, wives; kids and babies. Two families that were getting bigger by the month. From all over Dublin and some from England. A boyfriend from Limerick, one of my cousin's. He sang The Night They Drove Old Dixie Down later on. My father is smiling. So is Carmel. It was the only time my father smiled that day, I think; he always smiled for the camera. Denise is squinting. My mother is looking at my father. My brothers look like dwarfs beside Charlo's. The weather was nice; bright. Denise isn't the only one squinting. The photographer had us all looking bang into the sun. He was a dreadful eejit.

—Say cheddar.

It was chilly as well; you can see it in the way people are standing, one or two on Charlo's side glaring at the photographer. A stranger looking at the photos could tell where one family started and the other ended; it's like a border running through the middle of the pictures. Different sizes, different faces. My Granny O'Leary died two weeks after the wedding. She looks fine in the photographs. She looks the same age as my mother. She never liked my mother; I always knew that. The old man beside her is my Granda. He died last year, long after my father. I hadn't seen him for a long time before he died. I got out of the habit of going to see him; I'd begun to like him less and less, so I stopped.

I'll put the photographs away now so I don't start going through the rows, counting the dead. It was a good day. That's the word: good.

—I do.

I wasn't pregnant. So there. It was love. Love and my father. He didn't want us to go with each other — he hated Charlo, called him a waster, a criminal, a skinhead, a hippy — so we got engaged. To spite him. A great cluster of jewels to wave under his nose.

—Look, Daddy!

Bought in the Happy Ring House. I met Charlo outside. I saw him standing there before he saw me, when I was coming up from the bus stop. God love him, he looked mortified. I rubbed it in, spent ages looking in the window and pointing the rings out to him. This one, that one. I was worse inside. I tried them all.

—I love a bit of glitter.

The look on his face when he saw the prices; he couldn't believe it.

—It's only a bit of metal!

He whispered it into my ear when the man was bending over another tray.

—The jewels as well, Charlo, I said.

Cash. He handed it over. He'd saved up for it. No one had cheques or cards then. I never did, ever. Charlo had a good job then, for McInerney's; Charlo built most of the northside. Every time we met he'd tell me that he'd been working on the house we were going to get. He wanted to live out in the country, where Darndale was.

—Great for the kids, he said.

Then he blushed. He had it all worked out, and so did I. He saw the same future that I saw.

It wasn't just to spite my father. We were in love. I was mad about him. He was mad about me; he was. He loved me. He loved being with me. We laughed. He cuddled up to me. I could make him go hard just by staring at him. He lived for the times when I was with him; his face lit up. There was one grin that was all for me; his mouth and his eyes, his teeth over a chunk of his bottom lip, as if he was trying to fight back a laugh. He saved up for the ring, stayed at home so he wouldn't spend the money. He ate chips out of my knickers.

—Take your knickers off.

Out of the blue. He sounded like he'd just had a great idea; he couldn't wait to show me. It wasn't threatening or nasty. We were outside the chipper, midnight or later.

—Charlo!

—Go on, he said. —I want to show you something.

—No.

—It's not what you think, he said. —You'll like it; go on.

130

—No; fuck off.

—Go on, he said. —It's nothing to do with sex or anything like that; don't worry. I'd do it for you. Paula; go on.

There was a lane beside the chipper.

—Hold my chips, I said.

He held his hand out.

—You're not to eat any.

—I have my own, he said.

—Just don't, I said.

—Hurry up, he said.

I brought the knickers back to him balled up in my fist.

—Hang on, he said.

We walked on a bit, away from people.

—Give us them here, he said.

I gave him the knickers in exchange for my chips.

—Look it.

He held the knickers on one palm with his fingers coming out one of the leg holes. He upended his bag so that some of the chips fell onto his palm, onto the gusset. He handed me the rest of his chips.

—Now look.

He took a chip off my knickers and ate it.

—Jesus! Charlo!

He ate another one. He winked at me.

—Lovely.

After I started laughing I couldn't stop. He was laughing as well. He got all the chips into his mouth.

—There now, he said.

Little bits of chip sprayed out of him. He couldn't stop laughing.

—I ate chips out of your knickers, he said. —You'll remember that for the rest of your life.

131

He handed them back to me.

—Mind the vinegar when you're putting them back on, he said.

I had to marry him after that. Although we were with each other for a year before we got engaged. And another year before we got married. Jesus, I was happy. We were both happy. Both of us dying to get out of our houses and into our own — a room, a flat, a box, anything. Anywhere. Fitzgibbon Street, Coolock, Darndale. Australia. We talked about going there. He wanted to go; I didn't. I wanted to go; he didn't.

—Christmas at the beach.

—It wouldn't be the same.

We'd go over Europe and Asia, through India. There was something called the Magic Bus. We'd save enough money and take our time. We'd hitch and go on the roof of a train.

—The Taj Mahal.

—McInerney built that as well.

We'd go through Burma and China.

—That'd be the business.

We'd drop in on Chairman Mao for a cup of tea. We'd spend the winter in Shanghai, then we'd head south for Australia and the rest of our lives.

It was so far away; we'd never see anyone again. It was too far. We both had jobs here. There were housing estates being built all over the place, all around the city; the papers were full of ads for skilled labourers — just turn up at the site and ask the foreman. The city was bursting with people growing up and getting married. There were people coming home from abroad. No one was leaving any more. Charlo had a criminal record.

—Talk to them, I said.

—Talk to who?

—The people in the embassy, I said. —You're different now. You were only a kid. They'll see. You're a
good worker; they'll want you.

Summer in the winter. Upside-down. Aborigines and
Skippy. We didn't go.

We didn't want to. We didn't need to. We were happy.
We had money. We could see the mountains from the
roof of the flats we were moving into. We were in love.
Our whole lives ahead of us.

My father walked me up the aisle. He had to hold
me back. I just wanted to get up there. To get to Charlo.
I rested my hand on his arm. His sleeve was stiff and
cold. He'd said nothing to me in the car to the church.
Just the two of us. There was a separate car for the
bridesmaids, my friend Dee and my sister, Denise. (It
couldn't be Carmel because she was older than me.
And Wendy was getting over the chickenpox, so she
wouldn't do it. Dee didn't mind being asked three days
before the wedding.) Daddy's chance to bury the hat-
chet, to wish me luck, to say that the weather had stayed
nice for us; anything. No, though; nothing. He sat in
his morning suit like a chicken in tinfoil, looking out
the window. He never as much as looked at me; I had
to open the car door for myself. He made sure we
weren't touching. Our house was only a hundred yards
from the church but the chauffeur brought us twice
around the estate to make a journey of it. People waved,
children ran alongside us. I smiled back out at them
but all I knew was that my father was beside me miles
away. He said absolutely nothing. It killed me to think
that people could see him staring out at them, on his
daughter's wedding day, on his way to the church, on
his way to giving her away.

It was good in a way, though. I couldn't wait to

stop being Paula O'Leary, to become Paula Spencer. I wanted nothing to do with the O'Learys again. My father, Carmel; they were bitter and warped. They hated happiness. I was finished with them, gone. They'd see me at Christmas and that was it. The wedding was my great escape and, best of all, the grumpy old fucker was paying for it.

Charlo was up at the front waiting for me. With his brother, Liam, the best man. He smiled at me. I think he was smiling at my father as well. He knew my father hated him and he didn't care; he loved it. He smiled at me. His eyes got bigger. He was admiring me; he thought I was gorgeous. And I was. Nearly running to get to him.

—Here comes the bride —

Ninety inches wide —

He looked gorgeous as well. Born in the suit. Straight-backed and comfortable. A smile that would have made Elvis jealous. A smile that said I love you and I want to rip your clothes off. A smile that said We're going to live happily ever after. He believed it. I believed it.

I was standing beside him. I laughed, and stopped myself. Some of the stuff getting out of me; the happiness and excitement. My father was somewhere behind me. Charlo was looking at me.

—I do.

Paula Spencer. The new me. The adult. Just twenty and married. Married to Charlo Spencer. The man with a past and a future. The man they all wanted. The man I got. The man who chose me.

There was confetti. There were cans tied to the back of the car. And Just Hitched in shaving foam. We ran to the car through the guests and neighbours. Showered with the confetti. Pats on the back and thumps for Charlo. The photographer missed it; we did it again. The chauffeur gave out about the shaving foam; it burned through the paint. Charlo told him to shut up. We kissed in the car. Tongues. Nearly in public, stopped at the lights.

—Let's skip it, said Charlo.

—What?

—The dinner and that, said Charlo.

—No, Charlo.

—Come on.

—No way; it's my wedding day.

We kissed again. He hadn't meant it. He was as happy as I was. He leaned nearer the chauffeur.

—How much do these things cost? he said.

—I don't know, said the chauffeur. —I don't own it.

He didn't like talking.

—I'll get you one, Charlo told me.

He leaned out to the chauffeur again.

—How much are your wages, pal?

I laughed and laughed and looked at the driver's neck going red.

Photographs of me and Charlo pretending to cut the cake. Me with his family. Him with my family. Us with both families. All of us smiling. Me with the brides-maids. Him with his brother. His brother with the bridesmaids. Leaning into Dee, ignoring Denise. It was my day. Being kissed by everyone; buzzing all around the place. Making sure that everyone was happy. I hardly saw Charlo, except at the dinner — the breakfast. Our table was up on a platform; me and Charlo, our parents, Liam, Dee and Denise, the priest. Prawn cock-tail. I looked around; most people weren't fussed about it. Charlo loved prawns. Then turkey and ham. Very nice. Sprouts, carrots, roast potatoes or mash, or both. I remember the taste of the gravy on the potatoes; I think I do. The cutlery whacking off the plates. Everyone stopped talking, only the odd word between mouthfuls. Sitting between Charlo and my father. Daddy ate it all. My mammy beside him, adjusting the food on the plate, busy but eating very little. Charlo's mother concentrating on her food. His father.

—Blotting paper, wha'.

All the brothers. The wives and girlfriends. Big people squashed along the long table. The priest. I can't remember his name. A real lemon-sucker. O'Hanlon, I think. Father O'Hanlon. Grace before meals, grace after meals. All the aunties still wearing their hats. Charlo pointed at the plate with his knife.

—Grand.

People stuffing themselves.

Then the pavlova.

—Fuckin' hell.

Lovely. Really special. Cream on top of cream. Chunks of hidden fruit. Pears, grape halves, tangerine segments. Everyone moaning, gasping. Watery mouths.

—Oh Jesus.

And there was more for those that wanted it. The waitresses were grinning. Their high-sided steel trays were full of good news.

—Here, love!

People started to panic; there couldn't be enough for everyone. First come, first served.

—Over here!

Chairs scraping, hands waving. Even the priest looked scared that there'd be none left. Charlo laughed. There was enough for everyone. The clink of spoons, tongues shoving cream back, swallowing. Everybody happy. More big men on Charlo's side; big women on mine. His mother was big. Big boned, not an extra pick on her; like a teenage swimmer. Her hair free. A big sexy grandmother. She opened her mouth and chewed. She disgusted my father. She frightened him. Tea and coffee; the speeches.

—Hush hush!

—Loads of hush.

—Shut up!

Liam walloped his pint with a fork. The telegrams; the ones I remember. Best wishes, all the way from my Auntie Doris and Uncle Jim in Long Island; don't forget your hammer, from the lads on the site with Charlo; don't do anything we wouldn't do, from the girls in H. Williams where I worked.

—And now, said Liam. —I'm calling on Mister O'Leary to say a few words; Paula's da.

He stood up. They clapped.

—I'm not used to talking like this —

—Says you!

He coughed.

—It's been a lovely day so far, thank God. We've just had a lovely meal; the best.

Applause for the staff and the food.

—The best of luck to Paula and Charles. He's a lucky man.

—Hear hear!

—So's she!

Laughing.

—Thank you all for coming and I hope you all enjoy the rest of the day.

That was it.

Applause.

Word for word.

—Good man.

He managed to say it all without looking at either of us — no fond look, no toast. He was no hypocrite. A pity; I wish he'd pretended. It would have been better. I'd like to have smiled back up at him, to have felt his hand on my shoulder, to have let myself get weepy.

Liam stood up.

—Loads of hush. Would the Spencers ever shut up!

—Good man, Liamo.

—Now Father O'Hanlon has a few words he wants to say to yis. Put your hands together for Father O'Hanlon.

The priest said something about the family rosary; I can't remember exactly. Something about if we were ever in trouble we should get down on our knees and say the rosary, it would sort out our problems. (I tried it; it didn't.) He said that we were a lovely couple and that we'd have lovely children.

Then it was Charlo's turn. He stood up slowly, uncurled himself and got taller and taller. Everyone watched him and admired. He smiled. He enjoyed being looked at. He was happy; I could feel it off him.

—Ladies and gentlemen, Father O'Hanlon, Ma.

Laughter.

—Yis all know me —

—More's the pity!

Charlo's lovely grin.

—I'm a man of action, not words.

—Yeow!

—Watch out, Paula!

My father beside me, looking into his tea. Charlo leaned down and took my hand.

—This is the best day of my life.

Then he kissed me.

Cheers, laughter, and clapping.

—He kissed me in a way I'd never been kissed —
Before-ore —

He kissed me, leaned over me and kissed me bang
on the mouth. Then he sat down without letting go of
my hand. His grin turned into a laugh. I can see it; he
was so happy. I'd made him that way.

—I do.

Into the bar. Chatting and laughter. My mother grinning and nodding like a mad woman — making up for
my father. The Spencers took over most of the tables.
They were wedding veterans. The men at the bar
handed glasses and mixer bottles over their shoulders
and heads, and back, hand by hand, to the tables.
Pockets full of notes. It was great to watch. They were
a real family, a great sponge of hard men and women.
I was one of them. I liked that. You were safe when
you were in there with them. You were welcome. They'd
die for you. They were funny and impressive. The
women with the women and the men with the men.
Charlo's mother sat there in the middle. She had her
head to the side and she nodded, like she was listening
to confessions. His father was up at the bar, handing
back the drink, pint after pint after pint of Guinness. I
sat in with the women. They smiled, made sure that
my dress didn't get creased or stained. A rum and black
appeared in front of me; they knew what I'd want. His
mother nodded.

Liam leaning into Dee. He winked at me.

The band and the dancing. Me and Charlo had to
get up first.

—Knock three times —
On the ceiling if you wa-want me —

I remember letting my head drop onto his shoulder,

139

just for a little while, to let him know I loved him and how happy I was.

—Twice on the pipes —

If the answer is no-ho-ho-oo —

Everyone stood around us and clapped. Then little cousins started running and sliding and his parents were dancing, and mine, Liam and Dee, and everybody. The band were brutal but Charlo liked that.

—Fuckin' hopeless, he grinned.

The Virginians. Orange shirts and waistcoats. Four of them. The drummer was my father's second cousin. He threw up his sticks and caught them.

—These are the dreams of an everyday housewife —

Jackets off, ties loosened or gone. It was still bright outside. The windows were fogged, little rivers running down them. I could taste the pavlova.

—An everyday housewife who gave up —

The good life —

For me —

Mixed with the gravy. We were circling too fast, like in a ceili. It didn't suit the song. I was sweating and dizzy. But it went. The taste and the terror. I laughed. Charlo whooped. We stopped and swapped, me with Liam, Charlo with Dee. Liam pressed into me. He licked my neck. I didn't have time to be properly shocked. Then he stood away and laughed.

—Indiana wants me —

But I can't go back there —

Me and his father.

—Did you see the price of the drink in this place?

—Is it dear?

—Fuckin' desperate. Still though, it's only the once. Y'enjoying yourself?

—Yes, thanks.

—Good. It's your day.

(I could never decide if I liked him or not. He came over to me at the funeral and held my hand for a while. Liam spat on the ground in front of me.)

—By the time I get to Albuquerque —

Me and my father.

—Are you enjoying yourself? I asked him.

—Yes, he said.

—Great, I said. —Thanks; it's been lovely.

Nothing back.

—I'll never forget it.

Nothing.

(The man at the wedding has killed the other father I had, the one I had when I was a girl. I can't get at *him* any more. I can picture him, no problem, even smell him — but he isn't my daddy. He's another man. He's not real. I don't trust him or myself; I'm making him up. He couldn't be the same man who was at my wedding, the same man who wouldn't come to Nicola's christening ten months later because he had a cold, who wouldn't take her in his arms when she was handed to him, pretending he didn't realise what was expected.)

Singing. It was dark outside. The Night They Drove Old Dixie Down. The Men Behind The Wire. All Kinds Of Everything. Going Up To Monto. Charlo's da sang Ain't Nobody Here But Us Chickens. He became a chicken on the stage in front of the band; they couldn't cope with him. He was brilliant. I looked around to see if my father was watching. He wasn't there. My Auntie Fay sang Ave Maria. Charlo's brother, Thomas, sang Brown Sugar.

—How come you taste so goo-wood —

He was great.

—Yeah — Yeah — Yeah — Woooo —

His lips and his shoulders. Spinning and ducking. All the Spencers were great actors. They were queuing up for their turn. I sang Vincent. I closed my eyes and dragged myself through it.

—Look out on a summer's day —

Wrong notes all the way through and silence in front of me. I finished, mortified and wet. They clapped and cheered. I fell off the stage to get away. Then it was Charlo. He knew thousands of songs. He only had to hear a song once and he could give it back and fill in the gaps with words of his own, better words. He never sang the same song twice. (Then he stopped singing. About ten years ago.) Everyone watched him. It wasn't just a song; it was a whole show.

—There's —

No lights on the Christmas tree —

Mother —

They're burning Big Louie tonight —

I knew the song. The Sensational Alex Harvey Band. Charlo loved Alex Harvey. He even looked like him when his hair wasn't combed. He had a few striped t-shirts like Alex Harvey's. He looked out over the microphone; he never looked at it. He stopped, pressed some words, and skipped over others.

—There's —

No elec-tricity —

Mother —

They're burnin' Big Louie tonight —

The Spencers were in charge now. My crowd were huddled in corners, sipping their drinks and waiting for going-home time. The Spencers had taken over. They even took the instruments off the band, got in behind the drums and started messing with the knobs on the amplifiers. The brothers. Liam, Thomas, Gregory, Harry, Benny and Charlo.

The wedding was over. I was married now, one of them. They were finished with my family. Not just the brothers. His mother and father, all his aunts and uncles and cousins. They took over the whole place. They kept on singing.

—I'm in lurve — huh —

I'm all shook up —

My crowd started leaving. They crept along the walls. There were cousins whispering behind me; a fight going on in the men's toilet. Harry started bashing the guitar on the floor. The Virginians stood beside the platform, looking at the brothers wrecking their gear and pretending it was great gas.

I went up to the room upstairs and sat on the bed. I wanted Charlo to come in now. Before it was too late. Before he got too drunk. Before he went off somewhere with the brothers. If he came in now it would become our wedding day again. I waited. I had my bouquet. I wanted to stand on the stairs and throw it and laugh. I lay down on the bed. It was cold. I got under the bedclothes without taking my dress off. I waited for Charlo. I listened to the noise.

22

I stood outside his house. In the drizzle. The house was in a swerving cul-de-sac, a lovely quiet place with a smell of the sea. I stood there for I don't know how long; a few minutes. I just wanted to see. I wasn't going to knock on the door, nothing like that. He was in there. There was a light on and his car was parked on the slanting drive. Pointing at the house, slanting down. A nice-looking car; stylish, silver-blue. My hair was like a cap on my head; the rain and drizzle had hardened it.

I was standing outside Mr Fleming's house. I was by myself. I'd got off the bus in Malahide and walked the rest of the way because I didn't know how far from the town his house was. I asked the way, and walked. Past the tennis courts and the Grand Hotel — we'd been to a wedding there once — and Oscar Taylor's restaurant, all the places named in the newspapers. On along the Coast Road. The estate name was carved into a piece of stone on the side of the road.

I didn't want to see him.

But I did. I wanted to see him doing something; putting something in the bin, cutting the grass, something ordinary. Something to prove that he was getting over it. But I didn't think I'd be able to look at him; I didn't want him to see me. I couldn't have looked at him. It had nothing to do with me, I'd have shouted. He left mc long before it happened. I didn't kill your fuckin' wife. He hit me too, you know. He hit me too. I'm sorry, I'd say. I'm sorry for your troubles. I'm sorry, I'm sorry. I'm sorry.

I'd only seen him in photographs. At the funeral, with his hand over his eyes. Coming down the steps of the court during Richie Massey's trial; looking thinner and older. I'd never seen him on the telly. I'd made sure I hadn't. I saw nothing on the telly after the first night.

I didn't see him this time. He didn't come out; I saw no movement inside. I was happier that way, but a bit unsettled, not ready to leave. Waiting. It wasn't a big

144

house. A very neat red-bricked bungalow. It had a name, a wooden plaque beside the front door: The Haven. Charlo had stood in the porch down there, waiting for the door to open. The net curtains on the windows stopped me from seeing anything; I wasn't going to go down the drive for a better look. I wondered had she put them up or had he, after she died. They were good for closing him in; that was what he wanted. He was in there.

The sea was behind the house. I couldn't see it from where I stood. All the houses blocked it; the row of little bungalows keeping the view for themselves — they'd paid for it. I imagined him looking out at the sea and the island, sitting back in a nice chair. A big window in front of him. Did it make him feel any better? Lambay Island. It really was a lovely place to live.

It was so quiet. I'd never been anywhere so quiet. Even the birds were silent. Maybe it was the drizzle. Maybe there weren't any. Maybe they were waiting for me to go. They didn't know me. I wasn't wanted. I'd been standing there too long; I didn't know how long it had been. I didn't know why I'd come. Just to see. To fill something in.

I walked to the end of the cul-de-sac. There were cars in front of most of the houses. People in; someone was looking — there had to be somebody. Looking at a wet woman in her daughter's jacket. There was a small park at the end of the road and another road at the other end of it, to the left. That must have been where they'd parked their car, Charlo and Richie Massey. I wasn't going to go over there. (Does blood leave a stain on cement?) In front of me, to the right, over a bunch of bluey-green trees, there was a beautiful house, like a castle. A really beautiful thing with two round roofs shaped like cones. And windows in them. A gorgeous-looking place. People lived in that. There was a weather cock on top of the highest roof. It wasn't moving. I don't think I'd ever seen a weather cock before, or noticed one. Arrows pointing four ways. People lived in there, had bedrooms in that roof. The trees in the park were in round groups. They looked old but the place seemed brand new. No cracks in the paths. no dog dirt. I looked over at where I thought Richie Massey had parked the car. I could feel nothing. I wouldn't go over. There was a lane beside the castle. Steps down to a small road above the main road. I could see the sea and the sand now. I went down the lane; it looked open and public. Strange trees that made me feel that I wasn't in Ireland. Even with the rain. Even the daisies were different. They were bigger and fuller, absolute flowers. There was a smell of things growing and dying. I came to the end of the lane. The tide was out. It was lovely; miles of shining wet sand and a mist that was thin enough to make things look more interesting. Lambay was floating by itself. There was a town off to the left, maybe Skerries, shaped like an American city in the mist. There were dunes made for Arabs. The railings were silver and lit. Hardly anyone around; a few people in parked cars, looking out where I was looking. Maybe thinking what I was thinking, feeling the same way.

I was happy. It made me happy to think that people lived here, in all this, with all this. In this quiet, with this view of the island and the sea and its fresh smell. Charlo had been here but he'd left nothing; I couldn't feel him anywhere. He'd been washed away. He was stuck to other places but not here. Mr Fleming was looking out his window. I decided that. He definitely was. He was looking out at the same view I was looking at. He was fine; lonely but fine. There was a woman in his bank who was in love with him, but he didn't know it yet. She was nice, mature; she'd be good for him, bring him out of himself, make him laugh. She'd respect his memories. She wouldn't compete. He stretched his legs and bent down to pick up his mug of coffee.

There was a bus stop near but I walked past it, and the next two. I was glad now I hadn't seen him. It was better imagining him. It made more sense.

23

We went to Courtown for our honeymoon. My idea. We had a week and very little money. The day after the wedding; the train to Gorey and a taxi the rest of the way. We said hardly anything, both of us wrecked from the day before, side by side, leaning into each other.

It had been the wedding day with no ending. There'd been no going-away. We were supposed to have changed into our outfits and pretended that we were leaving that night. I had a cream trouser suit; that's as much as I remember about it. There are no photographs of me in it. I think I had white shoes and a bag. Charlo had a jacket and trousers. It didn't happen. No down the stairs into the crowd of waiting friends and relations. No cheering. No kisses goodbye and dirty remarks. Charlo never came up to the room to collect me. I fell asleep. He came in at about three o'clock and blacked out before he hit the bed; I felt him landing. Our first full night together. No sex, no wrapped around one another. No synchronised breathing as we fell asleep together. I never threw the bouquet. It was the one thing I'd really been looking forward to. The triumph of it; I'm married and you're not, God love yis. I put the bouquet in the bin when I was tidying up the next morning, before we left for the train. Flowers first, stalks sticking up. I made sure it looked finished with.

I didn't mind it too much. I was married now and that was the important thing. My husband was lying beside me in the bed. My other half. His breath spread over my back; the first time we'd really shared a bed. I didn't mind it at all. It would be like this every morning from now on. Warmth and no rush; belonging together. The church had been great, and the meal after — the pavlova; Jesus — most of the day. Charlo was always very funny whenever he had a hangover. The sore head and stomach used to inspire him. He was hilarious. I waited for him to wake up. I was starving. I was gasping for a smoke but I didn't really want one. I never smoked in bed then; I had to be up and dressed first. He groaned and sank deeper below the covers. He knew I was there; he was doing this for me, a performance all for me. He was asking me to forgive him for the night before. And I did. No bother; it didn't matter any more. It was a laugh.

He sat up in the bed and looked around. He knew I was looking at him. He looked up at the ceiling, and around again. He closed his eyes, and groaned.

—Where's the fuckin' floor?

He pulled on his trousers, pretending at first that he didn't know what they were or how to get into them. He stood up, and dropped back. He went to the door and stuck his head out.

—I don't want to live here any more.

He left the door open. I sat in the bed and listened, his feet on the floor outside, heavier than if he'd been wearing shoes. He stopped, and I heard him, muttering for me.

—Wrong fuckin' way.

I heard him singing.

—I left my arse in San Fran —

Cisco —

We didn't stay in a caravan. I'd have liked that, just the two of us in a caravan made for eight, in an empty caravan park. There'd have been no log fire to lie in front of but it would have been lovely, the rain smashing down on the roof — there's nothing like rain on a caravan roof — and us inside, the curtains drawn and the wind to rock us. But it wouldn't have been quite right. Caravans were family things; there was nothing sexy or romantic about them, disappearing beds and water tanks that had to be filled. It would have been a bit weird, a honeymoon in a caravan, difficult to explain. Mind you, there was nothing sexy or romantic about the Bed and Breakfast we stayed in either. It was grand — clean and everything else — but it was nobody's love-nest. Mrs Doyle ran it; she owned it. She was a widow. She told us that before we got up to our room. She smiled at us when she opened the door. It was dark and raining. I sat on our case, fixing my shoe; the strap was killing me. *Our* case; our clothes mixed in together.

—You're a bit early for the sun, said Mrs Doyle.

—We booked, I said, in case she was telling us that they were closed. —Mr and Mrs Spencer.

—That's right, she said.

149

She was delighted when I told her that we were on our honeymoon.

—Ah lovely, she said. —Lovely. I could see you were a pair of love-birds. Not like some of the ones you get during the peak. Always shouting and roaring at one another and walloping the kiddies.

She stopped on the stairs and looked back down at us.

—I was married to Mr Doyle for twenty-seven years, God rest his soul.

—Is that right? said Charlo.

I was mortified. He was slagging her, I knew it; but she didn't notice.

—That's right, she said back.

She opened the door and stood back for us to go in before her.

—Now don't worry about any mess you might make, she said. —You'll only ever have the one honeymoon.

I liked her. She told me later in the week that she had a daughter married in Gorey — to a lovely little man — two sons, one in Dublin and one in London, both with good jobs in offices. She had seven grandchildren, and another little granddaughter who'd climbed into an old fridge dumped in a field near her house in Dublin and had closed the door behind her and suffocated.

—She'd be seven now, said Mrs Doyle. —Her birthday's tomorrow.

Charlo couldn't understand why I was crying. He put his arm around me and sat on the bed till I stopped but he didn't understand; I could tell.

—She might be making it up, he said.

—How can you say that!

—Well, she might, he said. —I think she makes up half the things she says.

He was right, but not about her granddaughter. Her birthday's tomorrow. You didn't make up things like that. It was too plain. Too simple. I've never stopped thinking about it. Everytime I open the fridge; I'm bending to get the milk and it lights in my head; almost every time. A fridge in a field. The luxury of it as well, being able to throw away a fridge.

I remember, I put all the underwear together in a drawer, Charlo's and mine, and then I changed my mind. I put his into one, and mine into the one under it. I put the case under the bed. He was lying on the bed, his hands under his head.

—The life, wha'.

I pulled back the curtain and saw myself in the window. I turned off the light; it was only three or four steps to the switch. I went back to the window and looked out; the back garden and next-door's back garden. I switched the light back on.

—Well? said Charlo.

—Well what?

—What can you see?

—The sea and boats, I said.

—Very nice, said Charlo. —Only the best. Come over here.

We lay there for ages in the dark and listened to the noises above and under us and outside. We heard feet.

—The jacks, said Charlo.

We waited. A door was opened and closed. We waited for a flush, waited to laugh. Nothing.

—Haha; you were wrong.

—Didn't flush it, that's all.

—Hasn't come out yet either.

151

—Nothing unusual there; give him time. He's in no hurry. He's on his holliers.

—How d'you know it's a man?

—Shut up.

Nothing; no steps, no flush.

—He's after dying.

I switched off the light. It was cold. It was actually fuckin' freezing. I knew our breath was coming out like steam in the dark; I could feel mine spreading above me.

—Happy?

—Yep.

—Very happy?

—Yep yep.

—Very very happy?

—Yep yep yep.

It was a wonderful honeymoon, start, middle and finish, all of it. We went for walks, we played the slots — we were the only ones in the arcade — we ate chips, we ate ice-creams — all in the rain. We had a few drinks every night — people began to nod hello to us — and we were up in time for the rasher and sausage every morning. We spent most of the time in bed — back up straight after breakfast. I worried about it a bit; I kept expecting a knock on the door or even Mrs Doyle barging in so she could clean the room. But she left us alone. And she always tidied the room. She must have been in a room somewhere, waiting for us to go out. She must have been listening. She always smiled when she met us.

—How're my newly-weds?

—Grand, thanks, Mrs Doyle.

—Lovely. You don't mind the rain.

—No.

152

—You haven't even noticed it.

—It doesn't matter to us.

—Lovely.

—That much.

She told us that she was giving us more breakfast than we were entitled to but she wasn't showing off and fishing for gratitude. She liked us. Charlo was great with her.

—Ah now, look at this, he said when she put the breakfast in front of him.

—Jaysis.

She laughed. She loved the way Dublin people talked. She liked this time of year the best. It got a bit too hectic later on; she couldn't cope with the noise and fighting back the sand.

—It gets into everything, she said. —I get them to shake their kiddies before they come in but it makes no difference. It's like hoovering the Sahara, so it is.

—D'you ever get to go on holidays yourself? Charlo asked her.

—Oh, I do indeed.

She went to her sisters' houses in England every October; Coventry one week, Luton the next. She put her feet up and let herself be spoiled.

—There's no sand in Coventry, she said. —I love it.

She had three brothers in America — Boston, Buffalo and San Francisco — and another one was dead.

—Cancer; cancer.

She hadn't seen her brothers in years. They didn't write. One of them was divorced and had re-married, a Mexican woman.

—Can you imagine it? She'd go down well here in Courtown. She looks lovely in the photograph.

I waited for her to get the photographs out for us but

she never did. Maybe Charlo was right; she was making it all up. She always went to Gorey for Christmas, to her daughter; except the Christmas after the little girl died in the fridge, when she went to Dublin.

—That's the Christmas I'd like to forget, she said. — That kind of thing ruins all Christmases. And my husband died on Saint Patrick's Day.

She started laughing.

—I've only Easter left.

The things I remember. The plates at breakfast. White with a yellow edge. I got the same plate two days in a row, the same chip. I wondered would I be given the same plate for the whole holiday. A stain in Charlo's underpants when they were on the floor. The shock of it, then the comfort: I knew him that well now; we were that close. The feel of the one-armed bandit as I pulled the handle towards me. The heat of the chips coming through the paper in my hand. A car light from somewhere going across the ceiling. The different creaks of the stairs. Mrs Doyle's Sunday clothes and her prayer book and beads. Standing on a sharp stone in my bare feet. Charlo throwing the stone into the sea and yelling after it to fuck off. Looking around to see if anyone had heard him, laughing. Rain. A swan in the harbour, looking miserable. The cold of the water when I paddled.

Nicola was conceived on the Tuesday night. I'm absolutely certain about that. I knew — I drew something into me. Something rushed into my head and made me slam my eyes closed, a mix of pain and happiness. She started then. Nothing will ever prove me wrong. I felt her. Then nothing for weeks, just the knowledge, waiting; what I brought home to Dublin. (I haven't told Nicola yet. I don't know if I ever will.

154

I'm not sure that she'd want to know; I don't know. I'll tell her some time when she's annoying me.) Sex all week. Me as much as him. I tired him out. Four, five goes a day. Twice after we got back from the pub. I'd never done it twice in a row before; I never knew you could. Neither did Charlo. It was never the same after, when we got home from the holiday; the sex. It was good but it was never the first time again. It wasn't the first time then either, strictly speaking, but it was the first proper time. Going to bed; waking up together. Not worrying. Feeling each other. Not hurrying. Lying cuddled up for ever and ever.

Before we got married it had always been a dash. Quick, before they came home, before it got cold, before the last bus. No no no, not here, not yet. Is there a smell? Is there a stain? Is there grass on my back? It couldn't be helped. We didn't have anywhere to go. It had to be quick. It had to end with him. He came, and we went. It wasn't his fault. He wasn't being a pig. The quicker the better. I liked the feel of him coming; I'd made him do it and we could get in out of the rain. Married, it was different. We didn't go anywhere when we were finished. We lay beside each other. We cooled down. We giggled. The noise of the bed, the squeaks and creaks, made us howl. I put my hand over his mouth. He held it with his teeth. It never scared me. He turned to me and held one of my tits.

—You're a ride, he said. —D'you know that?

—So are you, I said. —D'you know that?

—So are you. D'you know that?

I couldn't get enough of him. I was tired and sore but I didn't care. I didn't want to sleep. I wanted the ache. I wanted him in me, all the time. His weight on top of me. I wanted to squeeze him in further and further. I wanted to watch his face. I wanted his sweat to drop onto me. I wanted to drop mine on him. I got on top of him. I'd never done it before. I couldn't really believe it; I was doing this. I was inventing something. I held him and put him in. He felt deeper in me. I'll never forget it. I was in charge and he liked it. I held his hands down. He pretended he was trying to break free. I let my tits touch his face. He went mad; he bucked. He split me in two. I pushed down. I couldn't believe it. One of his fingers flicked over my bum. I did it to him. He lifted and heaved. I couldn't believe it. There was no end to it, no end to the new things. He did something. I copied him. I did something. He did it back. He took me from behind. I pushed back, forced more of him into me. I sucked him. He licked me. I made him come on my stomach. He sucked my toes. The whole room rocked and Mrs Doyle smiled at us every morning.

24

A post mortem by the State pathologist found that Mrs Fleming had been struck twice across the face but there was no evidence of a sexual assault.

He killed her when he saw the Guards coming. The shot was heard. By neighbours and some of the Guards on the Coast Road. A loud crack. Not what she'd have expected, one of the neighbours said. Maybe when he saw them coming over the wall at the back, from the kitchen window; men sliding soundlessly over the wall, experts. He panicked. The way they moved. There might have been sirens. He shot her. A shotgun. He blew her middle away. When he saw them coming. Experts coming over the wall. He panicked. She started shouting, screaming. His finger pressed the trigger. He'd never done it before. She was running at him, screaming. He did it before he knew what he'd done. She was dead before he understood it.

It didn't work. I couldn't convince myself. I couldn't deny or believe it. I hadn't a clue. I kept starting at the beginning and trying to get to an end, an ending that wasn't appalling. I wanted an ending that included the facts. There was only one big fact: he had shot her. No; there was another one:

. . . Mrs Fleming had been struck twice across the face . . .

Not slapped, *struck*. He'd struck her twice before he killed her. Why? He'd struck her hard enough for the State pathologist to say definitely what had happened. He'd left the marks, like places on a map. Two marks? Both sides? One on top of the other? Slapped, punched, kicked? Why? The papers didn't say. Why had he hit her? There'd have been no need — the sight of the gun and Charlo's eyes breaking through the balaclava would have been more than enough to stop her doing anything stupid. When he'd hit me he'd been keeping me in my place, putting me back in my box. I said there was a smell off his breath: whack. I signed up to do a night class, I gave him a too-soft egg: whack. I went to the doctor: whack. He followed me. There's nothing wrong with you; what's your problem? Whack. And I loved him when he didn't do it; I loved him with all my heart.

He was so kind. He just lost his temper sometimes. He loved me. He bought me things. He bought me clothes. Why didn't I wear them? Whack. But why did he whack poor Mrs Fleming? He wasn't married to her. He hit her twice. What had happened?

I wanted none of the answers that started to breathe in me; I smothered them. They were all horrible. They were all just savage and brutal. Nasty and sick. They mocked my marriage, my love; they mocked my whole life.

. . . but there was no evidence of a sexual assault.

No evidence.

What did that mean? Nothing. Had he struck her because she'd tried to stop him? To soften her up? The marks on her face *were* the evidence. Then he'd seen the Guards sliding over the wall. Then he'd shot her. Because she'd have told them. He'd shot her so she couldn't say anything.

No.

Yes.

No.

She was nearly the same age as my mother, only six years younger. The photographs in the papers, the same two again and again; she looked like the granny she was, a nice granny — old, round, finished. A shy smile — don't waste your time photographing me. He'd hit her because she started making noise. He'd panicked, or he'd just hit her to shut her up. There was *no evidence* because there was nothing else. He'd just hit her.

But she'd played tennis every day. She went swimming. She was active. She was very popular. She did things. She had her own car. She whizzed around.

Photographs were misleading; I'd seen some of me. I've seen bad ones of Nicola, and she's beautiful. You couldn't tell from photographs, especially in newspapers; they were spotted and dull, photographs of photographs. Mr Fleming would have given them the first ones he'd found.

I knew Charlo.

A woman alone. A challenge. A laugh. He was wearing his woolly balaclava; he was hidden, Superman. (He bought his balaclava. It was in the papers a few days later; putting the whole thing, all the events together. He bought the balaclava in Alpha Bargains on Liffey Street. He murdered a woman, he used a stolen shotgun, he tried to rob twenty-five thousand pounds, but he bought the balaclava. That was just Charlo all over. The fuckin' eejit.) Even if she was as old and dumpy as the photographs said she was. It didn't matter. It didn't have anything to do with it. Young men raped old women. It happened, it had happened before. The mother of a neighbour of mine was raped and nearly killed by a young lad of nineteen, out of his head on drugs, in her old-folk's flat. He'd broken in for money and he'd raped the poor woman, then beaten her up and left her for dead. It happened. Looks and age had nothing to do with it. Men raped women.

He'd killed her because she'd have told them. He weighed up his options; her alive, or dead. Then he'd shot her. Aimed. No panic. Right in the middle. He'd ripped her apart.

Yes.

It had happened that way.

Yes.

No.

Even if he had been doing something, thinking about

doing something — there was *no evidence* — he'd never have killed her just for that. He wouldn't have cared. He never cared when I knew that he'd been with other women, when I could smell them off him; he didn't care. He laughed; he denied it and winked. Just as long as I kept my mouth shut and didn't annoy him. He loved it; he thought it was hilarious. Some of those women were no paintings, and I'm not boasting; I was better-looking than most of them. I told him that; I couldn't understand it. And he laughed again. He'd have laughed at her when she was telling the police. He'd have looked at them; he'd have nodded at her. Will yis listen to her. The state of her. I can hear him. He'd have taken off the balaclava to show them his face. There was no evidence. He knew these things. He didn't know what embarrassment was. He'd have laughed right at her.

He saw the police. He panicked. He shot her.

Charlo never panicked.

He panicked this time, the first time in his life; he didn't understand what was happening to him. He saw them coming and it hit him, and she was dead before he knew what the sound of the shotgun was. He looked at her. Under the low roof, the noise shocked him. Guards running. Guns. Better-looking guns than his. He looked at her settling on the floor; her head hitting, and rising, and landing. The blood. The walls. The floor. The mess of her clothes. And he ran.

He ran to the front door. The smell of the gun had spread all through the house. He opened the door. He heard cars. The Guards weren't there yet; they were late getting to the front of the house. He ran. To the right, away from the approaching cars. A car turning into the cul-de-sac. Others after it. He ran away from them. To the end of the road and the castle-house. He could run; he was fit. He played football. The cars emptied. Wheels skidding, doors opening. He looked back. Uniforms and plain-clothes. Hiding behind the doors, gliding along the walls. Used to all this. After him. He ran. To the left, away, off the road, over the little park, to the other road, to the car, where they'd left it. He ran, slid a bit on the wet. The ground would have been soggy. He'd have worried about muck getting on his trousers; I knew Charlo. He wasn't as fit as he thought he was; too much drink and takeaways. He was gasping. Feeling heavy. The shotgun weighed a ton. The rifle. He didn't know how to run and carry it properly. They were after him. He could feel their feet when his touched the ground. He was near the car now. The driver's door was on the path side. Was it locked? No. He opened the door. He looked back.

—Stop!

What did they yell at him? Stop? Halt? Stick'm up? It never said. Hey, you with the shotgun. I don't know. It doesn't matter.

—Stop!

He turned and pointed the gun at them. They were coming up behind him now as well. He was surrounded, by the police and the car; the houses, the clouds and the facts. He pointed the shotgun at them. They stopped and dived. He got into the car. He got out again; he never shut the door. He was getting out. One leg out on the road; the other stuck inside, under a pedal, caught on the mat.

—Fuck it!

The shotgun pointing. Empty. They didn't know that.

One of them shot him. Two more bullets as he fell

out of the car. He was falling anyway, his foot stuck. The shots came too late to push him back into the car. He fell face first onto the path. He was dead. He must have really smacked it, face first, no hands out to break his fall. He was dead.

They covered him with a blanket.

There were no last words. Top of the world, Ma! Fuck, Jaysis or Hang on. He just hit the path. Bang; dead.

The State pathologist examined him too, when he was finished with Mrs Fleming. Did the balaclava stop any cutting and bruising? The papers didn't say.

25

He lost his temper. And he hit me. He lost his temper. It was as simple as that. And he hit me. He sent me flying across the kitchen. I hit the sink and fell. I felt nothing, only shock. And a spinning in my head. I knew nothing for a while, where I was, who was with me, how come I was on the floor. Then I saw his feet, then his legs, making a triangle with the floor. He seemed way up over me. Miles up. I had to bend back to see him. Then he came down to meet me.

—Y'alright?

His face, his eyes were going all over my face, every inch and corner. Looking, searching. Looking for marks, looking for blood. He was worried. His face was full of worry and love. He was scared. He skipped over my eyes. He turned my head and looked at the sides.

—You fell, he said. —I didn't —

I fell. He felled me. I'm looking at it now. Twenty years later. I wouldn't do what he wanted, he was in his moods, I was being smart, he hated me being pregnant, I wasn't his little Paula any more — and he drew his fist back and he hit me. He hit me. Before he knew it? He drew his own fist back, not me. He aimed at me. He let go. He hit me. He wanted to hurt me. And he did. And he did more than that.

I'm looking at it now but that isn't what I saw then. I couldn't have coped with it then, the fact that he'd hit me, plain and simple, he'd drawn back his fist and smashed me. Something had gone wrong.

I fell.

I'd been too near him; he hadn't realised.

He'd only been warning me.

He didn't know his own strength.

He had things on his mind.

Anything.

It wouldn't happen again. Anything. It wouldn't happen again. How could it? It had been a mistake. We'd laugh about it later. Remember the time.

We did laugh about it later. That night. And the time after that. And the time after that. Many other nights. Until I couldn't laugh any more. I wouldn't let myself. Nothing came out when I opened my mouth. Only pain.

What happened?

I said, Make your own fuckin' tea. That was what happened. Exactly what happened. I provoked him. I always provoked him. I was always to blame. I should have kept my mouth shut. But that didn't work either. I could provoke him that way as well. Not talking. Talking. Looking at him. Not looking at him. Looking at him *that* way. Not looking at him that way. Looking *and* talking. Sitting, standing. Being in the room. Being.

What happened?

I don't know.

Someone once told me that we never remember pain. Once it's gone it's gone. A nurse. She told me just before the doctor put my arm back in its socket. She was being nice. She'd seen me before.

—I fell down the stairs again, I told her. —Sorry.

No questions asked. What about the burn on my hand? The missing hair? The teeth? I waited to be asked. Ask me. Ask me. Ask me. I'd tell her. I'd tell them everything. Look at the burn. Ask me about it. Ask.

No.

She was nice, though. She was young. It was Friday night. Her boyfriend was waiting. The doctor never looked at me. He studied parts of me but he never saw all of me. He never looked at my eyes. Drink, he said to himself. I could see his nose moving, taking in the smell, deciding.

He told everyone. He even got to my mother before I did. I was pregnant. We were thrilled. Charlo was delighted. He couldn't sit down. He kept looking at me; he couldn't wait. And he told everyone. He was boasting, of course. Only just married and his mot was already pregnant. What a man. (We didn't know about sperm counts back then, or else Charlo would have had a magnifying glass out, counting his.) What an absolute man. It was nice, though. I loved watching him telling people. I was making him so happy. He'd put his arm around me. I'd feel his strength in that arm, and our future. We were going places, everything in front of us.

We were in our flat in Sherrard Street, just married and in love. We had it done up nicely, even though we knew we wouldn't be staying. The minute the baby was born we'd have our name down for a new house. That was what we wanted, kids and a house, a full house; we didn't mind waiting. It was nice, the flat — except for the smell when you came in the hall door downstairs, the warm, sweating smell of old cabbage and nappies. Even the damp patch in the living room had a pattern that made it look deliberate. Living room, bedroom, kitchen. We shared the bathroom and toilet with four other flats. There were some right dirtbirds and weirdos on our floor. I was always a bit nervous coming out onto the landing. There was one old guy living by himself at the back who really gave me the creeps. I remember the winter when I was pregnant with Nicola, the mornings; looking out the door to see if the toilet door was open, the cold dash across with the toilet paper; the freezing seat, wiping it first, other people trying the door; the dash back to the flat. The flat was different at first, almost exciting; I'd always lived in a house before. There was something cosy about it even though it was actually cold and there were neighbours above and below us as well as beside us; there was always someone coughing or shouting or shifting the furniture. And I liked living in town. We could walk down to the pictures in the Savoy or the Carlton. I loved walking down Gardner Street; I loved the view down to Talbot Street and the railway bridge. I walked and window-shopped. I made it as far as Stephen's Green once. I was glad to be away from my family, and his. We got the bus out to see them on

165

Sundays, first mine, then Charlo's. I hated those Sundays, although I liked seeing my mother. Sitting there watching my father holding back his rage; wondering what would happen when we left. He never relaxed. Charlo always came and drank his tea, ate his biscuits and never said a word unless he was asked. My father never looked at him. We'd stay until six. We'd get up on the first bong of the Angelus and go up to Charlo's parents. It was different there but sometimes as bad. I'd have to wait in Charlo's with his mother, until he got back from the pub with his brothers and father. (He'd stopped bringing me after we got married.) We'd have to dash for the last bus back to town. I had to make sure I wasn't caught alone in the hall or bathroom or I'd get pawed by a brother. It was horrible; I was terrified Charlo would see something. I'd be blamed; I knew it. His mother was a strange woman. She'd say the odd thing but she'd never chat; the bare minimum.

—There's your tea now.

—Milk.

She'd shove a packet of biscuits across the table to me.

—Go on.

She wasn't being unfriendly. She just didn't know how to be friendly. Except when she was with her sisters and, sometimes, her daughters; at weddings and funerals. Then she was much livelier, in the middle of things. Then you'd hear her laughing. It was easier with the telly on; we didn't have to talk. A film. That's Life. And finally, Cyril.

The rest of the week was our own.

Charlo came home with paint and sandpaper and nails. He wouldn't let me help him. Not in my condition. A Thin Lizzy poster in the kitchen. We had a telly, a big old one with only two knobs on it that took ages to warm up. We only had rabbit's ears so we were stuck with just R.T.E. But we didn't mind; it was all temporary. (He tried to link up to somebody else's aerial, somebody up the stairs. He ran a wire out the window and disappeared for half an hour, but it never worked. It only had the two knobs, and one of them was only for the sound. You could only turn it on or off; there was no choice. He got annoyed for a bit and called whoever it was upstairs a dozy bastard, but it didn't matter. We'd soon have a roof of our own and we'd be able to hang an aerial off our own chimney. He only got annoyed because he thought he'd made a show of himself.) We watched telly; we went out for walks, the odd drink, the pictures. One Flew Over The Cuckoo's Nest. Dog Day Afternoon. The Big Tree was our favourite pub, or sometimes we'd go down as far as the Abbey Mooney. I loved the high ceiling, the painted fruit and leaves in the corners; it was absolutely gorgeous.

—Stop staring at it. They'll charge us extra for the drink. We laughed a lot, all the time.

He always came home. He always looked like he'd run at least part of the way. He did a lot of overtime, especially in the summer months just after we got married. He'd come in late, but never with a smell of drink off him. Not that I was checking. I got a bit lonely, surrounded by other people's noises. I'd turn on the telly and the radio and make noise of my own. I'd hear the key in the door and my heart would explode. He'd come in tired and smiling, dirty from work and hungry. He'd have his dinner on a tray. We'd talk. We were very, very happy.

I was pregnant. Was I sick? I don't remember. I was

proud; I remember that. I felt useful, like I was starting something important. Like I was working. I must have been tired and low at times, I must have been. I have clear memories of being exhausted and nauseous when I was carrying John Paul, and feeling and looking really good when I was having Jack. I remember crying when I knew I was pregnant with Leanne. I didn't want her at all; she wasn't welcome. I didn't want to go through it all over again. I can remember the exact feeling, seriously thinking about killing myself. But I can remember precious little about the first one.

I have a theory about it. Being hit by Charlo the first time knocked everything else out of me. It's all I remember now about that time, up to the birth. It became the most important thing. It became the only thing. One day I was Mrs Paula Spencer, a young wife and soon to be a mother, soon moving into a new house, in a new place, making my husband's dinner, timing it so it would be just ready for when he came in from work and had a wash. I was a woman listening to the radio. I was aware that my tummy was pressing into the sink as I was washing the spuds. I could feel the sun on my face, coming through the kitchen window. I had to squint a bit, squeeze my eyes shut; they were watering. I was a young, attractive woman with a loving, attractive husband who was bringing home the bacon with a smile on his handsome face. I was loving and loved, sexy and pregnant.

Then I was on the floor and that was the end of my life. The future stopped rolling in front of me. Everything stopped.

—Make your own fuckin' tea.

That was what I said. That was what started it, what ended it. I wonder what would have happened if I

168

hadn't said it, what would have happened if I'd gone over and put on the kettle.

—Make your own fuckin' tea.

Me and my big mouth. I'd have made him his tea. And a cup for myself as well. We'd have sat in the living room, me in the armchair we'd got from one of his cousins, and him on the floor. We'd have sat and chatted. He'd have made us another cup. I'd have been tired — I was always tired; I remember that much. We'd have gone to bed. We'd have listened to the neighbours downstairs fighting and the fairy from upstairs bringing in a new boyfriend. I'd have gone to sleep with his arm around me, my bum parked in his lap. I'd have slept like a log. Tomorrow's just another day. And the one after that. And the one after that and the rest of my life, the rest of our lives. Up to today. Now.

—How was work, love?

—Fine.

Kiss.

—Ready for a cuppa?

—Yeah thanks; I'm parched.

But I'm only codding myself. I know it. It would have happened anyway. That fist was always coming towards me.

—Make your own fuckin' tea.

But sometimes I can't help thinking that I could have avoided it, I could have been cleverer. I could have made that fuckin' tea. I'd done fuck-all all day; it wouldn't have killed me. He'd had his moods before. I'd seen them. I recognised them. I should have seen it coming. Instead, I provoked him. And now, here I am.

—Make your own fuckin' tea.

Now here I am, making my own fuckin' tea, buying my own fuckin' tea. Filling my big fuckin' mouth with tea. If I was in India or Africa I'd be picking my own fuckin' tea. A thirty-nine-year-old widow-woman with a hollow leg. A wreck of a woman with gaps where her teeth should be and a hole where her heart should be. A ruin, a wreck, a failure. What if I'd made that tea?

No, I'm only messing, codding myself. Feeling sorry for myself. (I haven't been drinking, by the way.) I know. It had nothing to do with the tea. It was coming all the time. The fist. The boot. The end. It had nothing to do with me.

I was tired and angry and sweating. My back was beginning to hurt. I'd gotten big with Nicola very early. I'd read nothing; I knew nothing about it. I thought I was carrying some sort of a monster. I didn't know about water retention or anything. My mother told me nothing. I was completely clueless, just pregnant and scared. I was jumpy and exhausted and miserable. The day had crawled. No one to talk to; nowhere to go to, too tired to go anywhere; all those stairs to get down and up, I couldn't have been bothered. Half-scared that the baby was going to come any minute. Premature and two-headed. A huge yellow-skinned oaf with a head too big to stay upright. I was ugly, fat and full of someone else's hairy body. My leg hair had gone black. I'd cried all day. I wanted chocolate. I wanted someone to bring me chocolate.

(I keep blaming myself. After all the years and the broken bones and teeth and torture I still keep on blaming myself. I can't help it. What if? What if? He wouldn't have hit me if I hadn't . . .; none of the other fists and belts would have followed if I hadn't . . . He hit me, he hit his children, he hit other people, he killed a woman — and I keep blaming myself. For provoking him. For not loving him enough; for not showing it.

170

For coming between him and John Paul. For not making love, for making love when I didn't want to. For not talking to him, for not understanding. For drinking and getting old. For not looking after myself. For throwing him out. For killing him. I can dismiss them all. It's easy; they're all unfair. I'm innocent, completely innocent. But they keep coming back. What if? His brother spat at my feet at the funeral: I was to blame. *Have you had a drink, Mrs Spencer?* The doctor in Casualty. It was settled: I'd slammed the door on my own finger. John Paul looked at the bruises on my face and he hated me. *Did you fall down the stairs, Paula? Did you walk into a door, Paula? What made him do that, Paula? What made* you *do that, Paula? Did you say something to him, Paula?* No. No. No! I'm innocent. I'm innocent. I'm innocent. What if he hadn't hit me then? What if I'd been more cheerful? What if I'd made his fuckin' tea?

No.

It was always coming. Before that night; before we got married; before we met. That was Charlo.

Why did you marry him then, Paula?

Fuck off and leave me alone.

He. Hit. Me.)

I was feeling low that night. I was feeling low and slimy. Low and slimy and mean. I was fed up and pissed off because he hadn't come home. Again. He hadn't been coming home for the last month. Since I'd started becoming seriously pregnant. Since I'd started looking wet and fat and white. *Why didn't you make the effort, Paula?* He came home later and later with drink on him. *Could you not have had a nice dinner waiting for him, Paula?* He'd say nothing to me. *Or the fire lit?* He'd grunt his answers when I tried to get us talking.

171

It had been bad for a good while. The honeymoon hadn't lasted long. He still came home, but sat staring at the telly. He wouldn't look at me. Then he came home later. Then later. Drunk and dirty from the site; he didn't even wash himself. Sometimes he'd come in straight after work, smiling — shy looking — as if he'd decided to start all over again. I'd be thrilled, every time; madly in love. It never lasted, though. There were always rows again. Even before we got married. He got worse. He'd pick rows with me for nothing. Why wasn't I wearing a smock his sister had given me? *Could you not have been more considerate, Paula?* Why had I set the alarm clock wrong? *Could you not have been more careful, Paula?* Why was the floor so dirty? *Well, Paula?* Where's my tea? *Well, Paula?* Make your own fuckin' tea. *Well now, Paula.*

I couldn't give him what he wanted, a pregnant wife who wasn't really pregnant. He saw me expanding and wilting and he couldn't handle it. He wouldn't. He wanted a baby but he didn't want anything to do with getting it. I was no good to him, an insult to him. Temporary wasn't a word he understood. He wanted nothing to do with me the way I was now. He hated what he saw. He hated me. (I'm so wise now, so handy with the analysis. I make it up as I go along. It's all shite. I change my mind every day.) I told him I'd soon have my figure back, after the baby was born. I tried to say it cheerfully, like I'd just thought it up, like I wasn't responding to his eyes. I'd backed into him in bed the night before, trying to make him hard. I wanted to feel him getting bigger against me; I was trying to prove myself wrong. I wanted to prove that I could still make him do it, that he wanted to do it. He loved me. I wanted him to ride me, to fuck me; I didn't care how.

He pushed me back and turned away. He said nothing. I went into the living room to cry. He was snoring when I went back in. There was no room for me in the bed the way he was lying. I had to get a corner for myself and push with my feet. I lay on the bed. It was cold and I was sweating. I don't think I slept. I made his sandwiches for him the next morning. He took them and went. He kissed me goodbye.

—Take care of yourself, he said.

I stayed in the flat all day. I spent most of the time deciding whether to visit my mother or not, until it was too late. I was too tired and heavy. I was restless but I didn't want to move. I was afraid to move. He came in that night. He'd been drinking. He wasn't drunk, though. It wasn't that late. *We all do stupid things when we're drunk, Paula.* He wasn't drunk. He even washed himself, a sign that he wasn't drunk. He changed his t-shirt. He still had some of his summer tan. He shaved. The two of us in the kitchen. He whistled. All The Young Dudes, I think it was; an impossible song to whistle. I felt bad now. My imagination had led me astray. Everything was fine. We were happily married. But I wanted to say something.

—Where were you?

—Campions.

I had to say something definite. I had to let him know.

—Nice?

—Yep.

He dried his face with a tea towel. He sat down at the table. I stood looking at him. He looked at me. He looked straight at me. It was a good, honest look. I was feeling so bad, so mean.

—Well? he said.

173

—Well what?

—The dinner.

—There isn't any.

He laughed. There was no anger in it, no shock, no sarcasm. He was so nice. He looked at the cooker and at me again.

—How come?

He looked away.

—I didn't know if you'd want any.

—What?

—I didn't know if you'd be home.

I didn't know if you loved me. I didn't know if you cared. I didn't fuckin' feel like it. I got it all wrong. I'm a cow. I'm a useless cunt.

—I'm here, amn't I?

I felt bad.

—Amn't I?

—Yeah.

I was a lump, a cow. Of course, he was here. After a hard day's work. Waiting for his dinner.

—It's just, I said. —It's just. You didn't touch it last night. And —

—I wasn't hungry last night, he said. —And now I am.

—Sorry, Charlo. It's just hard to tell.

I had to say something to him, something about the other times. I wasn't inventing things.

—What's that supposed to mean?

—I don't know what to do. I didn't know if you'd be home tonight. Like last night. I don't know where I stand with you, Charlo. I don't.

—Stop talking shite, will yeh.

—I'm not.

—You are.

—I'm not, Charlo. I mean it.

—Mean what? At least make us a cup of fuckin' tea. There.

He hit me. He sent me across the kitchen and I hit the sink and fell. I felt nothing, only shock. A spinning in my head. I knew nothing for a while, where I was, who was with me, what I was doing on the floor. I saw nothing; I was empty. Then I saw his legs, making a triangle with the floor. He seemed way up over me. Way up; huge. I had to bend back to see him. Then he came down to me. I saw his knees bending; I saw his hand pulling up one of his trouser legs. I saw his face. His eyes were going over my face, every inch, every mark. He was worried. He was shocked and worried. He loved me again. He held my chin. He skipped over my eyes. He couldn't look straight at me. He felt guilty, dreadful. He loved me again. What happened? I provoked him. I was to blame. I should have made his dinner. It was my own fault; there was a pair of us in it. What happened? I don't know. He held my chin and looked at every square inch of my face. He loved me again.

26

Ask me. Ask me. Ask me.

Here goes.

Broken nose. Loose teeth. Cracked ribs. Broken finger. Black eyes. I don't know how many; I once

175

had two at the same time, one fading, the other new. Shoulders, elbows, knees, wrists. Stitches in my mouth. Stitches on my chin. A ruptured eardrum. Burns. Cigarettes on my arms and legs. Thumped me, kicked me, pushed me, burned me. He butted me with his head. He held me still and butted me; I couldn't believe it. He dragged me around the house by my clothes and by my hair. He kicked me up and he kicked me down the stairs. Bruised me, scalded me, threatened me. For seventeen years. Hit me, thumped me, raped me. Seventeen years. He threw me into the garden. He threw me out of the attic. Fists, boots, knee, head. Bread knife, saucepan, brush. He tore out clumps of my hair. Cigarettes, lighter, ashtray. He set fire to my clothes. He locked me out and he locked me in. He hurt me and hurt me and hurt me. He killed parts of me. He killed most of me. He killed all of me. Bruised, burnt and broken. Bewitched, bothered and bewildered. Seventeen years of it. He never gave up. Months went by and nothing happened, but it was always there — the promise of it.

Leave me alone!

Don't hit my mammy!

I promise!

I promise!

I promise!

For seventeen years. There wasn't one minute when I wasn't afraid, when I wasn't waiting. Waiting for him to go, waiting for him to come. Waiting for the fist, waiting for the smile. I was brainwashed and brain-dead, a zombie for hours, afraid to think, afraid to stop, completely alone. I sat at home and waited. I mopped up my own blood. I lost all my friends, and most of my teeth. He gave me a choice, left or right; I chose left and he broke the little finger on my left hand. Because I scorched one of his shirts. Because his egg was too hard. Because the toilet seat was wet. Because because because. He demolished me. He destroyed me. And I never stopped loving him. I adored him when he stopped. I was grateful, so grateful, I'd have done anything for him. I loved him. And he loved me.

I promise!

I promise!

Don't hit my mammy!

I loved him. He was everything and I was nothing. I provoked him. I was stupid. I forgot. I needed him.

I buried a baby because of him.

He burned money in front of me.

—How will you cope?

He slashed my good coat.

—Where'll the money come from for a new one?

He picked me up off the ground. And I loved him. He picked me up and held me. He cried on my head. I needed him. For years I thought that I needed him, that I could never recover without him; I was looking for everything I got. I provoked him. I was useless. I couldn't even cook a fry properly, or wash a good shirt.

I promise!

I was hopeless, useless, good for fuckin' nothing. I lived through years of my life thinking that they were the most important things about me, the only real things. I couldn't cope, I couldn't earn, I needed him. I needed him to show me the way; I needed him to punish me. I was hopeless and stupid, good for only sex, and I wasn't even very good at that. He said. That was why he went to other women.

—Can you fuckin' blame me?

I could smell them off him. He called me other names

when we were in bed. He rubbed me and called me
Mary and Bernie. He laughed. He closed his eyes and
called me Chrissie. I could see him looking at them.
Knackers and dirtbirds. Bleach and false teeth. He
came home with their smell on him and then he had
me. For afters. He even came home with lipstick on his
collar. It must have been deliberate. The lousy bitch,
whoever she was. The lousy cheap bitch, kissing his
collar. She must have known.

I lost a child because of him.

There were days when I didn't exist; he saw through
me and walked around me. I was invisible. There were
days when I liked not existing. I closed down, stopped
thinking, stopped looking. There were children out
there but they had nothing to do with me. Their dirty
faces swam in front of me. Their noises came from
miles away. There were rooms, food, clothes — nothing.
There was a face in a mirror. I could make it smile and
not smile. There was a warped, bruised face. There
was a red-marked neck. There was a burnt breast.

Leave my mammy alone!

I promise!

I promise!

There were days when I couldn't even feel pain. They
were the best ones. I could see it happening but it
meant nothing; it wasn't happening. There was no
ground under me, nothing to fall to. I was able not to
care. I could float. I didn't exist.

The second time he hit me he grabbed my hair and
pulled me to him. I saw him changing his mind as he
hauled me in. His grip loosened. He stared at me and
let go. Another mistake; he hadn't meant it. I saw it in
his eyes; that wasn't Charlo. Charlo was the one who

178

let go, not the one who'd grabbed me. I can't remember why; I can't remember exactly when. I was still pregnant. Sunday morning, before we went to mass. I can't remember why. Something to do with breakfast, but I'm not sure. He was talking to me, giving me a lecture or something. I looked away, began to raise my eyes to heaven. (That was a habit he beat out of me.) I felt the rush and the sting on my ear, the air exploded and I was yanked forward. I stepped quickly to stay on my feet. My ear was hot and huge. I might have screamed. My skin was coming off the side of my head. I stepped forward, and looked at him. My hands — the palms landed on his chest. His face changed. He let go of my hair. I said nothing. I watched his face. I wasn't scared now; I hadn't time to be. He took his fingers out of my hair. He might have wiped them on his trousers. I watched him. He looked caught, cornered. He said nothing. He backed off. The side of my head settled into a throb. The left side; I can still feel it. He went into the kitchen. He said nothing. No sorrys, no excuses. I wish I could remember it all; it doesn't matter. I could make it up and it would still be true. He'd hit me again. We went to mass together. He bought me a Flake on the way home. I used to break them before I unwrapped them. Then I'd open the wrapper very carefully, slowly and I'd take out the bigger pieces, then the smaller ones. Then I'd make a funnel of the wrapper and empty the chocolate dust into my mouth. He watched me while I did it. I didn't offer him any. He smiled. I was making a fool of myself. He liked that. I was his little fool. I didn't care. His smile meant lots of things. I smiled back. Over and done with; another mistake. We went to my parents' house. It was Sunday. He helped me off the bus. I was his pregnant wife. He walked at

179

my pace, crawled along beside me. We walked side by
side. We talked.

—Don't hit my mammy!

Leanne's voice. Leanne's arms around my leg, cling-
ing to me. Her fingers pulling a back pocket of my
jeans. Her feet under mine. As he went around me.
And I turned to keep facing him. Trying to keep Leanne
behind me.

—It's alright, love.

To Leanne. Patting her head. Her fingers pulling at
my pocket. Her face pushed into me. Looking at her
father. Looking at his fists. At his face. Her face pressed
into me, wetting me. Not being able to see her. My
hand on her head.

—It's okay.

Having to keep my eyes on Charlo. Pleading with
him, holding him back. Feeling Leanne's shivering.
Keeping him back. Making sure I faced him. Making
sure she stayed behind me. Making sure I didn't let her
become a shield. Her hand gripping my jeans. Her
heart beating. Keeping my eyes on Charlo's eyes.

He once asked me how I'd got my black eye. I didn't
know why, what he was up to. It scared me. We'd just
been talking, about something on the telly. We used to
watch the News; this was years ago. I think it was
during the Hunger Strikes. Charlo was big into the H
Blocks. He knew all the names, how many days they'd
gone without food; he was an expert. He'd have loved
to have been in there with them. I said that to him.

—Yeah, he said back.

He didn't even know I was slagging him. He wore a
black armband all around the place, put it on before

180

his trousers every morning. He still ate like a pig, though, and drank like one. We were watching the News, commenting on it, and he asked me where I'd got my black eye. I kept looking at the telly. I was being tested; I was sure I was. There was a right answer. But this came out of nowhere. There hadn't been a row. There wasn't any tension. We'd been getting along fine, chatting away about the world and the H Blocks. It was nice; the trick was to agree with everything he said. Then he came out with it.

—Where'd you get that?
—What?
—The eye.

It was a test. I was thumping inside. He was playing with me. There was only one right answer.

—I walked into the door.
—Is that right?
—Yeah.
—Looks sore.
—It's not too bad.
—Good.

He was messing with me, playing. Like a cat with an injured bird. With his black armband, the fucker. Keeping me on my toes, keeping me in my place. Pretending he didn't remember. Pretending he'd never seen black and red around and in that eye before. Pretending he cared. I didn't believe he'd forgotten, not even for a second. He wanted me to think that — or that he was sick, having blackouts, that he was like Doctor Jekyll and Mister Hyde, a schizophrenic, that I should feel sorry for him and try to understand. I didn't believe it. He was playing with me. Ruining the night because it was getting too cosy. Only playing. He had me; I could say nothing. I could never fight back. When

181

he wasn't hitting me he was reminding me that he could. He was reminding me and getting me ready. Like the cat playing with the bird, letting it live a bit longer before he killed it.

He put one of his fingers on the bruise. I made sure I stayed absolutely still. I looked ahead, at the telly. The tip of his finger was freezing. He rested it gently under my eye.

—You must have walked right into it, did you?

—Yeah; I wasn't looking.

—Which door?

—Bedroom.

He took his finger away. I could still feel it on my cheekbone.

—Were you drinking?

—No.

—Sure?

—Yeah.

—Just careless.

—Yeah.

—Okay.

I waited for more. I sat beside him and waited.

—I saw you.

—You didn't.

—I fuckin' saw you.

—You didn't, Charlo.

He's making it up as he goes along, making himself believe it; working himself up, building up his excuse. He's getting ready to let go. He's going to beat me; there's no point in arguing, nothing I can do. I should say nothing. But I never learn. I always defend myself. I always provoke him.

—I know what I fuckin' saw, righ'.

182

He's seen me looking at a man. In the pub; we're just back from the pub, just in the door.

—I didn't look at anyone, Charlo.

His open hand. The sting and the shock, the noise, the smack. He's too fast.

—Say that again.

You never get used to it. Predicting it doesn't matter. Nothing I can do; he has complete control. It's always fresh, always dreadful.

Again.

Always a brand new pain.

The skin doesn't get any harder.

Stay out of the corners; I have to make sure that I don't get caught.

Again.

Buzzing. Things swim and dive. My husband is beating me. A horrible fact. A stranger. Everything collapses.

—Say it.

Again.

A stranger.

—Cunt! Say it.

The back of his hand. Too scared to expect it. Shapes are changing. My hair is grabbed as the hand comes back. Stay out of the corner.

—You fuckin' cunt!

Pulls my head down.

—You fuckin' —

Pushes me, drops me into the corner. Hair rips. A sharper pain. His shoe into my arm, like a cut with a knife. His grunt. He leans on the wall, one hand. His kick hits the fingers holding my arm. I lose them; the agony takes them away. Leans over me. Another grunt, a slash across my chin. My head thrown back. I'm everywhere. Another. Another. I curl away. I close my eyes. My back. Another. My back. My back. My back. My back. Back shatters.

The grunting stops. Breaths. Deep breaths. Wheezing. A moan. I wait. I curl up. My back screams. I don't think, I don't look. I gather the pain. I smooth it.

Noises from far away. Creaks. Lights turned on, off. Water. I'm everywhere. I'm nothing. Someone is breathing. I'm under everything. I won't move; I don't know how to. Someone's in pain. Someone is crying. It isn't me yet. I'm under everything. I'm in black air. Someone is crying. Someone is vomiting. It will be me but not yet.

Do I actually remember that? Is that exactly how it happened? Did my hair *rip*? Did my back *scream*? Did he call me a cunt? Yes, often; all the time. Right then? I don't know. Which time was that anyway? I don't know. How can I separate one time from the lot and describe it? I want to be honest. How can I be sure? It went on for seventeen years. Seventeen years of being hit and kicked. How can I tell? How many times did he kick me in the back? How many times did I curl up on the floor? How can I remember one time? When did it happen? What date? What day? I don't know. What age was I? I don't know. *It will be me but not yet.* What is that supposed to mean? That I was nearly unconscious; that the pain was unbearable? I'm messing around here. Making things up; a story. I'm beginning to enjoy it. Hair *rips*. Why don't I just say He pulled my hair? *Someone is crying. Someone is vomiting.* I cried, *I* fuckin' well vomited. I choose one word and end up telling a different story. I end up making it up instead of just telling it. *The sting and the shock, the noise, the smack*. I don't want to make it up, I don't want to add to it. I don't want to lie. I don't have to; there's no need. I want to tell the truth. Like it happened. Plain and simple. *My husband is beating me up. A horrible fact. A stranger*. Did any of this actually happen? Yes. Am I sure? Yes. *Absolutely sure, Paula?*

I have a hearing problem, a ruptured eardrum. A present from Charlo. It happened. A finger aches when it's going to rain. Little one on the left; he pulled it back till it snapped. It happened. I have places where there should be teeth. There are things I can't smell any more. I have marks where burns used to be. I have a backache that rides me all day. I've a scar on my chin. It happened. I have parts of the house that make me cry. I have memories that I can touch and make me wake up screaming. I'm haunted all day and all night. I have mistakes that stab me before I think of them. He hit me, he thumped me, he raped me. It happened.

He pushed me back into the corner. I felt hair coming away; skin fighting it. And a sharper pain when his shoe bit into my arm, like the cut of a knife. He grunted. He leaned against the wall, over me. I heard the next kick coming; my fingers exploded. Another grunt, and my head was thrown back. My head hit the wall. My chin was split. I felt blood on my neck. Again. Again. I curled away to block the kicks. I closed my eyes. He kicked my back. Again. My back. My back. My back. The same spot again and again. He was breaking through my back.

The grunting stopped. He was finished; he'd no wind left. I could hear him breathing, slowing down. He was wheezing. I waited. I curled up, tried to push the pain away. I stopped thinking and waiting; I didn't look; I

185

didn't do anything. I tried to spread the pain through my body, to take it away from my back. I could hear whining and crying, breathing. It was me. I heard noises from far away. Charlo was going up to bed. Lights turned on and off. Water running. I stopped listening. I stopped everything. I was a ball in the corner.

I'm everywhere. I'm nothing. Someone is breathing. I won't move; I don't know how to. Someone's in pain. Someone is crying. It isn't me yet. I'm in black water; it's cold and soothing. Someone is crying. Someone is vomiting. It will be me but not yet.

He'd bring me a cup of tea. Or a Flake. That was all it took. A tiny piece of generosity — a kiss, a smile, a joke. I'd grab at anything. And I'd forget. Everything was fine. Everything was normal. He'd put the Flake in the fridge and let me find it. That took planning; the kids always had their heads in the fridge, especially at night — his timing had to be perfect. That was all it took. I still break them before I unwrap them. I sometimes cry when I eat them.

The doctor never looked at me. He studied parts of me but he never looked at my eyes. He never looked at me when he spoke. He never saw me. Drink, he said to himself. I could see his nose twitching, taking in the smell, deciding. None of the doctors looked at me.

I didn't exist. I was a ghost. I walked around in emptiness. People looked away; I wasn't there. They stared at the bruises for a split second, then away, off my shoulder and away. There was nothing there. No one looked; eyes stared everywhere else. I could walk down the street, I could sit in the church at mass, I could go up for communion. I could answer the door, I could get on the train, I could go to the shops. And no one saw me. I could stand at a checkout and empty my trolley, pay for what I was buying. I could hand over my money and get my change and stamps. I could push past people and let them pass me. I could say Please and Thank you. I could smile and say Hello. I could smile and say Goodbye. I could walk through crowds. I could see all these people but they couldn't see me. They could see the hand that held out the money. They could see the hand that held open the door. They could see the foot that tried on the shoe. They could see the mouth that spoke the words. They could see the hair that was being cut. But they couldn't see me. The woman who wasn't there. The woman who had nothing wrong with her. The woman who was fine. The woman who walked into doors.

They could smell the drink. *Aah*. They could see the bruises. *Aah, now.* They could see the bumps. *Ah now, God love her.* Their noses led them but their eyes wouldn't. My mother looked and saw nothing. My father saw nothing, and he loved what he didn't see. My brothers saw nothing. His mother saw nothing. Denise saw nothing — at first. (Carmel was living in England.) The woman who kept walking into doors.

—How are you?

—Grand.

Ask me.

In the hospital.

Please, ask me.

In the clinic.

In the church.

Ask me ask me ask me. Broken nose, loose teeth, cracked ribs. Ask me.

187

No one saw me. I was fine, I was grand. I fell down the stairs, I walked into a door. I hit myself with the heel of his shoe. I looked older than my age; what age was I anyway? It was my little secret and they all helped me keep it. He held me still and butted me. He dragged me around the house by my clothes and by my hair. Fist, boot, knee, head. He hurt me and hurt me and hurt me. (Carmel saved me; Carmel was the one. Carmel saw what was happening, and she made me see. And she made the others see. Carmel saved me and I've never thanked her. Sometimes I cursed her. It was easier when you couldn't feel or see.) I began to see what they saw. Nothing. I kept my eyes on the ground. I stopped looking at faces that were looking away from me. It was easier not to see them, and then I forgot why I didn't look. I shopped at the last minute, I wore a coat in the summer — I hid. I sent the kids to the shops. I wore plastic sunglasses. I drank. I avoided mirrors. I closed the curtains before dark so I wouldn't see myself in the window looking back in. I turned off. I forgot. I gave up.

The children made it difficult to stay that way. They always made me come back. I had to be there; I had to be visible for them. I had to think. I couldn't give up; they wouldn't let me. I had to be alive, awake and doing things. I couldn't die and leave them. I wanted them more than I didn't want them — and sometimes I didn't want them at all. But I couldn't leave them with him; I couldn't let go. They were there all the time. They had to be fed. They had to be hugged. They had to be cleaned. I had to be there. So I lived in the house. I was alive for them. They could see me. They could feel me. They'd grow up and then I could disappear. I could fold myself up and stop. But I had to be there for them until they were big enough. I had to protect them. He kicked me, he bruised me, he scalded me. Sometimes I hated them. He'd put them there to trap me; they were in it with him. They never stopped crying. They never stopped eating. They wouldn't let me lie down. They were on his side. They never left me alone. I always had to be there. I could never disappear.

When they were in bed or in school I could close down. I could curl up. After a hiding, after a fight, I'd curl up in a corner on the floor; I'd hum and concentrate on the humming until the aches became one pain, one pain that didn't change, that got no worse. I could feel the blood drying, becoming something else, something that didn't come from me. Then I could sink under the pain and there was nothing.

There was beautiful nothing, until I had to wake up and be myself again. The pain separated into aching limbs and muscle and I had to stand up and become Paula Spencer again. I had to straighten myself up and wash the dried blood from my face. I had to fix myself up and ignore the pain. I often woke up on the kitchen floor. The invisible woman. The woman who walked into doors.

—What made you do that?
Fuckin' doctors.
—What made you do that?
Stupid fuckin' bastards. What made me do that? Looking at my eye. Looking *for* my eye, behind the pulp. He didn't want an answer; he muttered, thought he was being nice. Silly you; look what you did to yourself. None of them wanted answers.
—A little bit of make-up will cover that up for you.

None of them looked at me.

—As right as rain.

None of them saw. Tut-tut-tut and another prescription. More pills to wash down. There was sometimes no food in the house but there was always valium.

—Do you take a drink, Missis Spencer?

Plenty of rest. Put your feet up for a while. Get your hair done; spoil yourself.

—Put this woman to bed the minute you get home, Mister Spencer, and bring her up a cup of tea.

—Yes, doctor.

The two of them, looking after me. Laughing at me. The woman who walked into doors. They didn't wink at each other because they didn't have to.

They were all the same; they didn't want to know. They'd never ask. Here's a prescription; now fuck off. The young ones were the worst, the young ones in Casualty. So busy, so important.

—It's people like you that waste my time.

I should have boxed her ears. A kid in a white coat, playing. Shouting at the nurses. A fuckin' little child with no manners. And I took it from her.

—Sorry, doctor.

—Next.

There'd be days when I'd wake up, when my head would be fresh and clear, when I'd feel tall and strong. My nostrils were long. I'd feel the air sailing up, cooling my head as it went. I tasted things. I wanted things. I'd hold onto the children. I'd feel them, look them all over. They grew in front of me. Their faces changed. They were good days. They'd climb up on me. I was awake. It was over. I'd clean. I'd wash. I'd try to catch up. I was doing it for him. To prove to him. I was worth it, worth loving. I worked and worked so the guilt couldn't catch up with me. I cut the grass. I made sure I knew what day it was. I worked. I washed. I cleaned the floor, the sink, the toilet. I washed sheets. I hung them out. I laughed when the wind whipped them back into my face. It was good to be alive. It was good to be in the back garden hanging up the washing. I made the beds. I ironed. I listened to the radio. I caught up. I brushed their hair. I sorted out their clothes. I made piles and filled the hot press. I put on lipstick and faced the world. I put in earrings. I polished shoes. I lined them up and polished them all. I tried to remember where they'd all come from.

He did love me. I know. He proved it again and again. Right to the very end. Even after I threw him out. It was just something in him. A bit of something that turned bad. Charlo was an angry man. The temper was always there, underneath. It was a good thing about him; he knew what he wanted, he got what he wanted. It was good to know that you were with him. Watching him, being with him. It was exciting.

If he'd been a bit different he would have been great at something — he'd have made a different name for himself. A businessman or a politician, or even an actor. He'd have been a star. If he'd had the education. If he'd had other work when all the building around Dublin stopped and there was nothing left for him to do. He would have put that anger to use. He wouldn't have been wasted. He'd have been a leader. I can see him. Managing a football team. Putting the fear of God into them at half-time. Standing up and speaking in the Dáil, tearing strips off the Minister for Social Welfare. Jumping out of a moving car — doing his own stunts.

Teaching problem kids. They'd have loved him. Vote for Charlo Spencer. Co-starring Charlo Spencer. Written and directed by Charlo Spencer. Scored by Charlo Spencer. But he wasn't unemployed the first time he hit me. Beaten by Charlo Spencer. That's a fact that I can't mess around with. Robbed by Charlo Spencer. Murdered by Charlo Spencer. Charlo Spencer lost his job and started beating his wife. It's not as simple as that. He started robbing. He shot a woman and killed her. Because he didn't have a job, was rejected by society. It would be nice if it was that easy. If I could just think back and say Yes, that was how it was. Charlo Spencer lost his job and started beating his wife. I could rest if I believed that; I could rest. But I keep on thinking and I'll never come to a tidy ending. Every day. I think about it every minute. Why did he do it? No real answers come back, no big Aha. He loved me and he beat me. I loved him and I took it. It's as simple as that, and as stupid and complicated. It's terrible. It's like knowing someone you love is dead but not having the body to prove it. He loved me. I know it. But if he loved me, why did he hit me? Why did he hit me so hard and so often? The questions are never answered. They always torment me. And his love becomes a cruel thing, like a smile on a Nazi's face. You don't hit the people you love. You might, once or twice — it's only human. But not the way he did it, again and again. You don't pull back their fingers till they snap. You don't wake them in the morning with a kick in the stomach. You don't hold their face over the chip pan and threaten to dump their head into the boiling fat. You don't beat them in front of their children. That's not love. You can't love someone one minute, then beat them, and then love them again once the blood has been washed off. I can't separate the two things, the love and the beatings. I can't say that he was like that some times and like this other times. I can't make two Charlos. I can't separate him into the good and the bad. I take the good and the bad comes too. I lie in bed curled up thinking of the good and I can feel the bad chilling my back. I remember us moving into our brand new house with its lovely smell of paint; I remember bringing Nicola and John Paul around — he was only a tiny little fella — and showing them all the rooms a few days before we moved in; I remember that it was Charlo who was carrying John Paul and I was holding Nicola's hand. I remember that it was a hot day in the middle of a hot week and all the muck of the unfinished roads and gardens had turned into dust. There was no bus to the new estate — it didn't really exist yet. We had a long walk from the bus stop. There was still a farmhouse. Nicola waved at the farmer in his tractor; I told her to. The man waved back. We didn't know where he was going with his tractor. His fields were gone. There was a big chestnut tree that the Corporation had left standing at the top of our road. Charlo said it was left there because the squirrels had an uncle in the planning department. I remember being too warm and very excited. I remember Nicola twirling around and pulling the arm off me. Is this our new house Mammy, is this our new house Mammy? I remember being a bit shocked even though I'd been here many times before. It was all raw and bare, the edge of the world. I remember being worried. I suddenly wondered what the neighbours would be like. I wondered how far it was to the nearest shop. I wondered would the place always look like an abandoned building site. I couldn't imagine it changing, growing older and smoother. There was a cement mixer, turned over on its side, in the front garden two doors up. There were kids playing in front of the houses that were already occupied. I didn't like the look of them. They were rough-looking, even the girls, filthy language coming out of them. I didn't want Nicola hanging around with them; I looked at her looking at them. The old tree was at the top of the road, though. The rest of the estate would catch up with it; it would be lovely. All kids were loud and rough. Their mammies could never keep them clean with the dust and dirt. Mine would be the same. And the house. I loved it. Finished and untouched, the walls bare and waiting. The smell of newness. This was it. Home. This was where we'd stay. (We'd moved flats four times. Too small. Too damp. Evicted because of the noise we were making.) The new smell of the new house would rub off on us. A new start. I remember: we'd brought the kettle, milk and tea, sugar in a paper bag. Charlo hummed the national anthem as I filled the kettle for the first time in our new kitchen. We got Nicola to clap when I turned on the gas under the kettle and it came on. Whoosh! It was a big day. I remember it all. How I felt, how I looked, Nicola's face, the smell of the house, the dust in the air, the taste of the tea.

—That's good water came out of that tap, Charlo said. —Only the best.

I remember Nicola loving the stairs, our own stairs — she didn't have to share it with anyone. She sat on them while we went from room to room. The sun reflected off Charlo's watch, a bright spot on the front bedroom wall. John Paul saw it and squealed and the two of them stayed there for an hour, playing with the light-spot on the wall, until the sun dropped away. Myself and Nicola went out to the back garden and decided what we'd grow there. Banana trees. I wasn't certain if bananas grew on trees. (I'm still not.) Nicola was positive about it. Potato trees. Orange trees. Gooseberry bushes.

—Trees.

—Bushes, love.

—Trees.

—Trees and bushes then. One for each of us.

It was cooler in the back garden; it was cold.

—I don't know if we'll be able to grow bananas on this side, love.

I remember everything about that day. (I don't remember actually moving in a few days later.) I remember it all. And I believe everything I remember. A new start. Warm on one side of the house, cold on the other. The taste of the tea. The packet of Kimberley biscuits. John Paul filling his little mouth with biscuit, and emptying it. Nothing to clean it up with. The smell of the house. The echoes. The toilet, using it the first time. Launching it, Charlo said. He left the door open while he went loudly on top of the water. Nicola sitting on the stairs, shuffling herself until she was nice and comfy. Scraping the tape off the new window in the kitchen with my thumbnail. Closing the door behind us when we were leaving. Not wanting to leave. Closing the door gently. Our new door. His hand on my back. Nicola's hands on my legs. John Paul asleep on Charlo's shoulder.

—I can't fuckin' wait, said Charlo.

I backed closer to him, agreed with him. We looked at the door, and up at the rest of the house. Then we went on to my parents' house — it was Sunday. Two buses. It started to rain. The four of us upstairs in the bus.

—Paddy on the railway track picking up stones, along came the train and broke Paddy's bones.

I remember everything; I'm sure I do. I remember it all, but I remember this as well: the pain in my arm where he'd pinched me the night before, the huge bruise that his finger and thumb had left. He'd made me follow him all through the flat, pulling me by the flesh of my arm. It was agony. He'd speed up and slow down, squeeze harder if I cried out or said anything. Because he wanted to do it. I don't remember the excuse. Because he could. The pain couldn't have been worse. What was the fuss; it was only a pinch. It was agony, out of nowhere. He dragged me for minutes. Until Match of the Day started. The music always reminds me. (There's still a mark there, on the inside of my arm, little red pinpricks left by his bitten nails.) I remember that Nicola wouldn't let him touch her. She was all over me. She never let go. I had to sit beside her on the stairs. She pawed me and held onto me all day. I remember being nervous. I remember being scared when it started to rain, that it would change Charlo's mood. I was worried that John Paul would get on Charlo's nerves. John Paul never rested when he was asleep. He squirmed all the time; it was impossible to get comfortable when you were carrying him. I remember closing my eyes when I saw the Kimberley biscuit and milk on the back of Charlo's shirt, deciding what was best, whether to tell him about it or not, terrified that somebody else would tell him first. Charlo wouldn't have cared, I know that, but at the time it seemed vital. I remember it. Everything was fragile and hysterically important. I was tired and gleaming from lack of sleep; my eyes didn't fit, my shoulders ached. I was sore from sex that I hadn't wanted. I remember

I wanted to get away; I wanted to run. I couldn't stand any more. But I didn't want to run. I wanted everything to be perfect; everything was going to be great — I just had to be careful. I was responsible for it all. The clouds coming, I was dragging them towards us; my thoughts were doing it. I was ruining everything. It was up to me. I could control the whole day. All I had to do was make sure that I made no stupid mistakes. Don't walk on the cracks. Don't look at the clouds. It's up to you. A lovely day and I hated every minute of it. Every step was into a huge black hole; there was nothing underneath me. Nicola's tears, John Paul's snotty nose, spilling the sugar onto the floor — everything made me panic. Everything was heading into disaster. Our chance for a fresh start and I was going to wreck it. Something I'd do, something I'd say. Anything. It would be me. Me and my big feet or my big mouth, my butter fingers or my fat ugly face. It would be me. I'd ruin it before we could start.

Stop.

That's the thing about my memories. I can't pick and choose them. I can't pretend. There were no good times. I can never settle into a nice memory, lie back and smile. They're all polluted, all ruined. Nothing to look back at that isn't painful or sick. My tongue explores the gaps in my mouth and I remember how I lost my teeth. Every day, every time I move my tongue. I move my shoulder on a damp day and I remember. I see packets of Kimberley biscuits stacked up in the supermarket and I remember. The tiny old bruises on my arm. The scar on my chin. Leanne wetting the bed. The smell of old cigarette smoke. The taste if I put too much sugar in my tea. The empty fridge. The creak in the fourth step of the stairs. The bell. Match of the

Day. The sun lighting up the kitchen at teatime in the summer. They all remind me. They all stab me. They laugh at me and never let me go.

Memories are made of this.

A taxi to the hospital. He held my hand and put his free arm behind my back to keep me steady, so my arm wouldn't bash against the door or the seat. He chatted with the driver. He was relaxed, in control, looking after me. They were talking about the Stardust; it had been a week since the Stardust fire. They both knew people who had died. They were sorting through them, trying to find out if they knew any of the same people. I listened to them. I knew people too but I said nothing. I didn't want to intrude. He was speaking on my behalf, for us both. His shock was mine, his opinions. I was always like that when Charlo was talking. I was happy listening to him. He had just pulled my arm out of its socket, less than an hour before, and I was listening to him; I was actually admiring him, proud of him. He'd run next door to get their young one, Ann, to babysit for us and to phone for the taxi. She thought we were going to the pictures. I was a mess but my coat was good.

—Which one are you going to see? she said.

—We'll see what's on when we get there, I said.

We saw the lights of the taxi pulling up outside.

—Are we off so? said Charlo.

—There's a bottle fixed up for John Paul in the fridge, I told Ann. —Remember to test it first before you give it to him, won't you. We won't be too long.

—Okay. Have a nice time.

It had been a long time since he'd hit me. I'd filled John Paul's bottle and screwed the lid on one-handed.

I remember being interested in how I was managing. I'd opened the fridge door, gone to the table for the bottle and the fridge door had shut by the time I got back with it. I put the bottle on the floor and opened the fridge again. I remember thinking about Mrs Doyle from Courtown's little granddaughter dying behind the fridge door. I was doing everything left-handed. He'd pulled out my right arm. I don't have to remember that. That noise is always there.

He opened the taxi door for me and got me in.

—Careful now, he said.

Him and the driver swapped names all the way, and stories of narrow escapes and tragedy. Charlo sounded like a spokesman for the area; the driver kept looking in his rearview mirror at him.

He always came with me. Always stayed at my side. Always brought me home after I'd been fixed up. Always looked after me. He gave the driver his money and tip before he got out of the car. Then he went round to my side and opened the door. The driver waited for me to get out. Charlo held onto my good arm. He bent down and spoke before he slammed the door.

—Good luck so.

He helped me into Casualty, almost did my walking for me. He sat and stood beside me all the time. He let me do all the talking and explaining. He smiled at nurses and doctors. He smiled apologetically when I told them that I'd fallen down the stairs. He was always there. I could see him on the other side of the curtain. I remember that night. I looked drunk and scruffy. My hair was greasy and flat — I still had it long back then. (I was still young.) Charlo looked well and smelt of the Old Spice my mother had given him for his birthday. You'd have felt sorry for him that night, being stuck with me. A drunken bitch who kept falling down the stairs and walking into doors. But he stayed by my side. He stood by me. He held my hand and patted my arm. He took full responsibility for me.

I'd been there before but it had been a good while. I knew some of the faces. I watched while I waited. I was in a daze, really. Drunk men and kids. A few women. I wondered why they were there. Waiting for their kids and husbands, I supposed. (Once, I heard a woman near me telling the nurse that she'd walked into a door, and I believed her. I felt sorry for her. Her eye was completely closed and in a state that didn't really have a colour, awful to look at. I couldn't take my eyes off it. She was in a very bad way, shaking and gulping. It never dawned on me that she was lying, the same way I always lied. I believed her completely; she must have been running when she hit the door, chasing after the kids or something. There were always other women there when I was there, waiting their turn like me, wounded women. I never once thought that I wasn't the only one who'd been put there by her husband. Seeing them there made me feel even worse; they were there because of honest accidents. I was there because of my husband's temper, because I'd provoked him, because I didn't deserve him. I envied them. And sometimes I hated them. They didn't know how lucky they were with their real accidents.) I knew some of the nurses. They came and went, did different shifts — left, got married — but I recognised some of them. (Maybe some of them had husbands who beat them.) I liked the nurses; I liked watching them work. They ran the whole show, really. They stayed calm and busy without rushing, patient with everybody. They were the life of the place. I wished I'd been a nurse.

—Fair play to them, said Charlo. —It can't be easy.

There was always a wait. I was never hurt enough to jump the queue. The crying and the moaning, the stretchers being wheeled in, seeing children tied to them — it took weeks to get it all out of my head. It was a mad place. Some of the people strolling around really did look crazy, staring at the ground, mumbling, holding onto arms that were bandaged, holding towels up to their faces. Some of them looked dangerous; broken, noisy people. I never saw myself in the middle of it. I was always on the side, not really there at all. Dropping in. There under false pretences. I felt ashamed, only myself to blame.

Sometimes it was different. Sometimes I'd think that I could escape if I could get behind the right curtain, if I was asked the right questions.

Ask me.

Charlo was always beside me, always near, but if I got the right doctor or nurse I'd be safe. They'd see, and they'd take me away. They'd take me through a door and I'd be gone before Charlo knew it. I'd have the kids out of the house before he got home. We'd be gone without ever having to look at him again. They'd help; they'd do it for me. There was a room up at the top of the hospital where we could stay, a place where he could never find us, with huge windows and a balcony. The right curtain. I just had to be in the right place in the queue. Open Sesame. I'd be led behind the curtain and it would be over. I'd be mended and safe. We'd be happy and safe. I'd get worked up waiting. I believed it was just a matter of luck. Maybe this time. A nurse would look at me and know. A doctor would look past his nose. He'd ask the question. He'd ask the right question and I'd answer and it would be over.

Charlo was always with me. He was always there. Behind the curtain was the only time I was alone. His shadow on the curtain. A few minutes. One question. One question. I'd answer; I'd tell them everything if they asked.

Ask me.

I'd have told them everything, I swear to God I would have. If they'd asked. I'd have whispered it. If they'd asked first. He pulled my arm behind my back and lifted me off the floor. It would have been easy after that, watching them listening. He hit me. He kicked me there. He burned me here. He did it. He did it. Save me. I'd have told them everything. I just had to be brought behind the curtain, asked the right question.

It was my turn.

—Mrs Spencer?

—Yes.

—Doctor will see you now.

I followed the nurse. She held the curtain open for me. She smiled. I'd seen her before; she had a new hairstyle. Charlo kept my coat. He followed me, as far as the curtain. I was in. I sat on a chair.

—Doctor'll be here in a minute.

I knew her; she'd seen me before. She was from the country somewhere. She looked at me. She nodded at me.

—In the wars again.

—Yes, I said.

She looked at her watch.

—Fell down the stairs again, I told her. —Sorry.

—You poor thing, she said.

She was nice. I didn't want to disturb her. She had a boyfriend of her own; she was bound to have. There was no engagement ring. Maybe he was saving for one, like Charlo had.

—In the dark, she said.

—Yeah, I said. —The bulb was gone.

—God.

It wasn't going to happen. It wasn't the right curtain.

—It'll all be over in no time, she said.

—Busy tonight?

—Sure, stop.

There'd be no escape. I could see Charlo's shape walking up and down outside. It would be fine later, when we got back home. He'd be great. I'd learnt my lesson. He'd bring me up a cup of tea. He'd get up with the kids in the morning, let me stay in bed. It wasn't so bad. It would be fine for a while.

The baby was gone before I knew if it was a boy or a girl. Between Leanne and Jack. Born too early; born by a fist. A girl. I never saw her. Her name is Sally.

27

It's all a mess — there's no order or sequence. I have dates, a beginning and an end, but the years in between won't fall into place. I know when I met him, I know our wedding day, I know the day I threw him out, the day he died. I have other dates — births, my father's death, communions, confirmations, other deaths. I can put them in a list down a page, but they're the only guide I have.

I missed the 80s. I haven't a clue. It's just a mush. I

hear a song on the radio from the 60s or 70s and I can remember something that happened to me; it has nothing to do with liking the song. Song Sung Blue — I'm doing my homework, listening to Radio Luxemburg, the chart show on Monday night, with Carmel and Denise. I'm drawing a map of Ireland, the rivers of Ireland. My blue marker is nearly wasted and I haven't got to Ulster yet. Lily The Pink — I'm sitting on my mother's knee, watching my Uncle Martin singing Delilah; I have a toothache. Somebody else sang Lily The Pink before or after him; I can't remember who — one of my cousins. All The Young Dudes — I'm watching Charlo washing himself at the sink. He still has some of his summer tan. But I don't know any songs from the 80s; they mean nothing — and the radio was on all the time. What did I do in the 80s? I walked into doors. I got up off the floor. I became an alcoholic. I discovered that I was poor, that I'd no right to the hope I'd started out with. I was going nowhere, straight there. Trapped in a house that would never be mine. With a husband who fed on my pain. Watching my children going nowhere with me; the cruellest thing of the lot. No hope to give them. They saw him throw me across the kitchen. They saw him put a knife to my throat. Their father; my husband.

—I do.

I was their future. That was what they saw. The grown-up world. Violence, fat and an empty fridge. A bottle of gin but no meat. Black eyes, no teeth; a lump in the corner. Do your homework, say your prayers, brush your teeth, say please and thank you — and you'll end up like me.

I never gave up.

Carmel told me to go. Fill a bag, get the kids and

go. Anywhere, her house, a refuge; go. She kept at me; I hated her for it. It was none of her business. She promised the police and barring orders. She was standing on me, making it worse, rubbing it in. There was nothing wrong. He'd be fine. He'd get a job and everything would go back to normal. He loved me. She just didn't like him; she was jealous. I was cruel to her. I shut the door on her. I threw things at her. (But she was there all the time. She was there when I wanted her. I've never thanked her.) I wouldn't go. I'd get to the door. I'd open it. No further.

The hidings, the poverty, the pain and the robbery. I never gave up. I always got up off the floor. I always borrowed a tenner till Thursday. There were always Christmas presents, birthday presents. They always had a Christmas tree. There was always some sort of food. I got between them and him. I guarded the fridge. I made ends meet.

I never gave up.

I'm here.

I picked myself up. I washed the blood off my face. I put on the kettle.

I came close. I wanted to die. I lay on the floor and felt death under it. It was warm and I wanted it. I never wanted to get up. I was broken; I wanted to melt. I didn't know who I was. All I knew was the pain.

But I got up. I always got up. I had children. I had a husband. I limped around the rooms, tucking the children up in their beds. I hung out the washing with a broken finger. I ate sugar and drank gin. I made sandwiches for their lunches; thin slivers of ham around the edges to hide the nothing in the middle. I hid. I hid the pain, the bruises and the poverty. The front door stayed shut. I went mad if one of the kids left it open. A knock on the door terrified me. I'd been seen, I'd been caught. I was guilty.

He beat me brainless and I felt guilty. He left me without money and I was guilty. I wouldn't let the kids into the kitchen after teatime, I couldn't let them near the cornflakes — and I was to blame. They went wild, they went hungry and it was my fault. I couldn't think. I could invent a family meal with an egg and four slices of stale bread but I couldn't think properly. I couldn't put a shape on anything. I kept falling apart.

The floor was warm and sticky. It was easier to stay there. It was nice. The blood hardened. It didn't want me to move. It wanted me to stay on the floor.

But I got up. Always, eventually. I'd remember who I was. I'd remember the time of day; I had things to do, things to look after. I'd mop the floor and start again. That was my life. Getting hit, waiting to get hit, recovering; forgetting. Starting all over again. There was no time, a beginning or an end. I can't say how many times he beat me. It was one beating; it went on forever. I know for how long: seventeen years. One stinking, miserable, gooed lump of days. Daylight and darkness. Pain and the fear of it. Darkness and daylight, over and over; world without end. Until I saw him looking at Nicola.

28

I stood at the front door so many times. I opened the door. I stepped out, into the garden. So many times. Never further. I changed my mind; I made excuses. I couldn't do it. I turned back. I'd go upstairs to pack and sit on the bed until it was too late. I'd let John Paul or Leanne or Jack have their nap first. I'd wait until I had some money. I'd wait until after Christmas. I'd wait until Charlo was asleep. I'd walk up to the door, gone already, just the door in the way. But I'd know; I wasn't going. There was nowhere to go; I couldn't go. I couldn't lift my hand to the latch. I couldn't go past the garden. I was walking into nowhere. Disgrace, the shame, the picture of him coming after me. There was too much; I had nowhere to hide. It wasn't worth it. Having to admit everything, nowhere to go. I'd pick up a piece of paper off the grass and walk back in, as if that was what had brought me out, one piece of paper, one out of all the papers and packets and plastic bottles littering the garden. (I once found a syringe in the grass, near the front wall. I didn't touch it. I didn't even think about it.) I'd walk back inside like I'd made my mind up. I'd feel better; this was the right decision. I'd stay. I was needed. It wouldn't happen again. I was better off with what I had. The kids needed their father. It wouldn't happen again.

He put the money on the table in front of me. I never got to count it. Or feel it. I'd been drinking; I was a bit slow. I'd been resting, sleeping. The kitchen, the light on — I was sitting up. Had my head been on the table? He picked up the money and put it back down again, now that he knew I was awake and looking. A wad of money. Serious money. Enough for clothes, enough for a big shop. A full basket full of lovely things, the kids with me, queuing up knowing that there'd be plenty left over when it was all paid for. A bit of excitement. Good lunches for school, lunches to be proud of — grins on their faces. Family packs of waffles and Mars

Bars. A jersey for John Paul with John Barnes' number on it. Shoes for Leanne. A tenner for Nicola. A bottle for myself. McDonalds Happy-meals for the lot of us, ice-creams with hot fudge after. A pile of money in front of me, a wad that would keep us going for as long as I needed to think about.

—There, he said.

Salvation and happiness. Out of nowhere. I looked at it. He watched me waking up. He watched me calculating, seeing the things I was going to get with the money. A pile that said hundreds. A pile that wouldn't get smaller unless you put in the effort. I was mesmerised. Very happy and wondering where the catch was. I knew he was watching. I didn't move. Bills gone, a full fridge full of family packs, pouring out of it when I opened the door. A trip to the pictures. A day in town and a taxi home. A real Sunday dinner, paper napkins and the works. Ah, Bisto!

He picked up one of the notes. A twenty. I didn't follow it. I kept my eyes on the rest. The twenty wasn't missing. The pile looked exactly the same. I didn't care where it had come from, how he'd got it. It was robbed; it had to be. I didn't care. The twenty-pound note came down again in front of my face. On fire.

—Look at that, he said.

He lit more notes with the flame. The blue notes turned black; black crumbs lifted into the air. He was setting fire to the lot of it.

—Isn't that a shockin' waste? he said.

I didn't answer him. He wanted me to. He wanted me to grab at what was left. Funny, I didn't care that much. It was interesting, watching it burn. It was so light. I followed the flame. But why was he doing this, making us broke again, him as well as us? I remembered: I'd told him I was leaving, that I wasn't taking any more. The day before, after he'd swiped at me for nothing. He'd laughed when I told him I'd get a job, that I didn't need his fuckin' money, that I could fend for myself better than he ever had.

He laughed now. He made himself laugh, like the baddy in a film.

—All that lovely dosh; it's a crying shame so it is.

He bent down and blew it off the table. I could hear the kids in the front room, fighting over the remote control. It was the first time I'd seen his face since he'd come in. There was nothing there, no cruelty. He was like a child now, studying his work. Not all the notes were burnt. He'd stopped; he left them on the table. He put five blue notes in front of me, one hundred pounds.

—Where would you be without me? he said.

He put his hand on my shoulder.

I could never get past the door. There were too many things. Things I didn't have. Money, somewhere to go. Too many things. The kids. The schools. People seeing me. All of them stopped me. It was all black out there. He said he'd kill me if I ever went. I knew he'd do it. He said he loved me and he couldn't live without me; he didn't care what happened to him after he'd done it, it made no difference to him, dead or alive, the rest of his life in jail, he didn't care — he'd kill me. I believed him. It was in his face and voice. He couldn't live without me, he said. He loved me. I couldn't go. He was sorting himself out. He'd come after me and kill me. And the kids. He said he'd never let me take them. I wasn't fit to look after them; I was only a fuckin' alco and too stupid. He wouldn't let it happen; they'd be better off dead. He looked at me. He meant it.

He smashed me against the door before I could open it. He hit my face off it. I waited for the glass to smash into me.

—I'll kill you; I'll fuckin' kill you!

I could never go.

I thought about it; I dreamed about it all the time. I made it up. I sat for hours, going from one step to the next. New house, a job, new hair and clothes. The kids in a new school in black school uniforms with a maroon stripe on their V-necked jumpers. A job in an office. I believed it as I sat there. I believed it all day. Me sitting at a computer. Working away at it, no bother. I always saw myself from a distance, hands moving but never the fingers on the keys. Or I'd see myself from the back of the computer, the camera rising over it. The light from the screen making two shining paths on my cheekbones. Starring Sally Field as Paula Spencer. Home from work — in my little car; I saw myself from the outside — I never had to learn how to drive. A neighbour waved, raking up the leaves. A huge room straight in from the front door, like Cosby's. Food for the kids, a microwave. Laughter, discussions. I helped them with their homework. I read them a bedtime story, all of us on my big fluffy bed. They went to bed together and they slept all night; no wetting, no crying out. I lived this life all day; changed bits, added others. I ran away all the time. I ran away to luxury. I ran away to a new face and body. Me and the kids, no one else. Me and the kids in a big sponge house. Miles from anything Irish. Couches. Rugs. A big white dog with no sex. Dry heat and warm snow. A fluffy dog that didn't shed its hair. A purple bathroom that I sometimes changed to pink.

I ran away in my dreams, the ones I could handle

and control. I didn't have real dreams, night dreams. I just went black. I didn't want the real ones. I drank myself into the blackness. I could never run away in the real dreams. I didn't let them in. Sometimes, though, they got through. I fought myself awake. I could never move; I couldn't breathe.

I ran away to twenty years ago. I ran away to another country.

He threatened me all the time, reminded me that I couldn't cope. I had nothing going for me. I was only Paula Spencer because of him. It was the only thing I was. People knew me because of him. We had the house because of him. I was there because he looked at me and proved it. One nice look could wipe out everything. I loved him with all my heart. I could never leave him. He needed me. He told me so, again and again. I was everything to him.

I always stopped at the door.

I was frightened of being without him. In the early days, I got excited when I heard him coming in at night, when I was lying in bed waiting for him; delighted he'd come home to me. At the same time I was scared. Would he be drunk? Would he be nice? Would I be awake or pretending to be asleep? I'd listen to his steps, reading them; how far away, how much drink on him, his mood. I could tell before he got to the room, but there was always hope. Happy feet — he was especially light on his toes when he was feeling frisky. I'd pretend to be asleep. That was the best, letting him think he was waking me. We'd make love for hours. On the bed, off the bed, in the hall. I'd feed the baby while his balls filled up again. Long, long ago. Excited and scared. Sometimes, I liked the mixture. Then it was just scared, no mixture. Just terror when the door slammed, terror all day. We had sex before he went out; I still wanted that, always. He loved me. I was mad about him. Behind that terror and cruelty, he was still there. But I had to get him before he went out. Then I could black out before he got home. If I was lucky.

If I was lucky.

I was so depressed I didn't even know there was a door there. I didn't know where I really was, or sometimes who I was. It was all nothing. Days disappeared. I'd wake up in the toilet. I'd stand in front the sink for hours, water pouring over the sides of the kettle — for hours. There was nothing to hang onto; everything was miles away. Sudden things made me cry. The bell, a door, a skid outside. I couldn't cope with anything coming at me. A letter dropping onto the hall floor. A bird squawking. Noises in the attic. I couldn't tell far from near, important from nothing. I cried when I heard the kids coming home; I couldn't love them — I couldn't concentrate on it. I couldn't cope.

Drink helped; drink calmed me. Drink gave me something to search for and do.

I'd wake up at three in the morning, wide awake. I'd crawl through the day. On good days I knew there was a door there. On good days I could dream. I could smile when I heard the kids coming. I knew where I was going; I knew why. I could love and think. I could feel miserable and know why. I could hate him. I could love him. The bad ones weren't days at all. They were mush. They were blank. Nothing. There was no door because it didn't exist. There was no dreaming. Someone was breathing. It wasn't me. I'd scream. It wasn't me. I was a black lump in the middle of a black lump. Nothing came near me; nothing got to me. There were children out there trying to get in. There were noises. I couldn't reach them. There were tears rolling down a face. There was no one there and no one watching. I was only someone when he walked in. Because he looked at me. Because he smiled at me. Because he hit me.

When was I like this? I don't know. Once? Always? I don't know. I can't arrange my memories. I can't tell near from far. I was married one day. I threw him out another day. It happened in between. That's all.

I threw him out! I'll never forget that — the excitement and terror. It felt so good. It took years off me. God, it was terrifying, though — after I'd done it, after I'd walloped him. I didn't think. I couldn't have done it if I had. But when I saw him looking that way at Nicola, when I saw his eyes. I don't know what happened to me — the Bionic Woman — he was gone. It was so easy. Just bang — gone. The evil in the kitchen; his eyes. Gone. The frying pan had no weight. I'd groaned picking it out of the press a few minutes before. It was one of those big old-fashioned ones. I hated it; a present from his mother. Maybe there was a secret message in it all along. Maybe that was it. When I saw him looking. It had no weight when I picked it up; I was being helped. I didn't feel the fat falling on me as I lifted it. Down — gone. *His* blood on the floor. My finest hour. I was there. I was something. I loved. Down on his head. I was killing him. The evil. He'd killed me and now it was Nicola. But no. No fuckin' way.

Down on his head. He dropped like shite from a height. I could feel it through my arms. He fell like I used to fall. All the years, the stitches, all the cries, the baby I lost — I could feel them all in my arms going into the pan. They lifted it. They were with me. Down on his head. It still makes me laugh. When I think about it. I couldn't go through the door, so I fucked him through it instead.

29

It was Thursday morning, a year before he died, two years ago. Why do I remember that it was Thursday? They were all the same — up, coffee, the kids up and out so I could sit down for a bit and recover, the first fag, the headache that lasted all day. Having to get up before the kids so they wouldn't eat everything — having to make things stretch, having to be mean. I hated the mornings. They upset me. I sometimes cried before I got up. It was just so hopeless. It wasn't laziness; I've never been lazy. It was uselessness, the feeling that there was nothing. Only the kids. But sometimes I didn't think of the kids. I couldn't even cry. The smell of the room, the damp. Looking for clothes. The pain in my head. And nothing for the rest of the day. Only the kids. Always up before Charlo. Always. That bollocks didn't know that toast was made from bread.

It was Thursday. It was early. Nicola was often gone to work by the time I got down to the kitchen. But not this day. She was there, having a cup of tea before she went for the factory bus, making sandwiches for her lunch. I even remember what kind. Ham. There now. Her own private ham that she bought for herself. Just the two of us. We didn't say anything. I didn't like talking in the mornings and making small-talk with Nicola was hard at any time of the day. She was a moody little bitch back then. It was a phase; I knew it

— I didn't fight it. I didn't like it though. I did notice that she was looking bad, white and unhealthy, not her usual self. It was always easy to see when something was up with Nicola, she usually looked so good. She looked bad that morning. She hadn't slept. She was unhappy. There was something wrong with her. She looked sad and skinny. I didn't think about it. She drank her tea. I made my coffee.

Then we heard Charlo coming down the stairs and suddenly I was all talk. I couldn't shut up. It was nerves, I know now. I was trying to hold back the fact that I knew. Talking shite, I was trying to make sure that nothing had happened, that nothing would happen, that everything was normal.

—I don't know where I'll get the time.

Where I'd get the time! Time was the only thing I ever had. Time was why I hated getting up and started, having to kill it.

He was in the room now.

—And I've to bring Jack back to the clinic.

I looked. Charlo was in the door. He was staring at Nicola. But, really, he could have been staring at anything, waking up. He'd been drinking the night before, the whole day before. We'd opened a bottle of vodka at dinnertime, just after the kids had gone back to school, only Jack left in the house with us. I often did that, bought a bottle to try and get him to stay in the house, so we could drink like a happy couple. Charlo was as shattered as I was.

—And Leanne wants her hair done for her birthday.

Nicola looked quickly at Charlo when she was putting the butter back in the fridge. He looked back at her, up and down. Jesus — looking at it. Up and down. That was the thing in his face that killed me: the hate.

It wasn't the way men look at women — I could nearly have understood that. It was almost natural, something to be careful about. But it was sheer hate. It was clear in his face. He wanted to ruin her, to kill her. His own daughter.

I spoke to her, to get her away from that stare. I really didn't know what to do.

—Nicola?

—What?

I kept looking. He didn't seem to care that I was there.

—Will you bring Jack to the clinic on Friday?

I don't think Nicola heard me properly.

—Yeah, she said.

She wasn't really listening to me. She got a half-day on Fridays — they got their pay at half-twelve and the factory shut. She'd never have given up her Friday afternoon. I'd only said it because it came into my head. I'd have said anything.

—Thanks; that'll be great.

I remember it word for word. I've no doubts about it. Second by second. I saw him. He wanted to hurt my daughter. His daughter. Because he could. There was evil in him. I wasn't going to pretend any more. Things were falling apart and it didn't matter. I looked at Nicola. She looked at me. Yes, her face said; you're right, it's happening. She looked embarrassed and guilty. What did I do? her face said. I'm sorry. Help.

He started humming. The noise disgusted me. The humming made me do it. I grabbed the frying pan. It was empty, just the fat. It wouldn't have mattered. He was looking straight at Nicola; he was going to make her get out of his way, rub against her. I could always tell when Charlo was about to move; his shoulders told

you. They went before his legs. I hit him on the side of
the head with the pan. Nothing stopped me. I didn't
care about damage or noise; my arm let me. His legs
went, he fell straight like he'd been hanged. He wasn't
unconscious.

—Paula — , he said. —Paula.

He sounded like a fuckin' eejit. Like a baby learning
the word. I knew I was angry now. I took aim this time.
He tried to get up. I hit him on top of the head. I could
have killed him; it didn't matter. He collapsed properly.

I felt great, so satisfied.

—I saw him.

I'd done something.

—I saw him, I said. —Looking.

Nicola nodded. She shut the fridge door.

—Is he dead?

—I hope so, I said.

He didn't matter any more; I'd done it.

—No, I don't, I said. — I don't care —

Then I began to worry. He moved and groaned. That
was what worried me. What next? I bent down to get
a good shot at his ear, to keep him down till I
thought a bit further. His head moved; I had to start
again.

—Kill him, said Nicola.

I didn't hit him. I straightened up.

—No, I said. —There's no need.

She couldn't believe me. She thought I was being
completely thick.

—He'll kill you now, she said.

—No, he won't, I said.

—He will.

—He won't; he's not that bad.

—Ah, Mammy —

She was terrified and getting angry with me. Here I was, letting her down after only saving her. I smiled at her.

—Don't worry, love, I said.

I let her see that I was relaxed, in charge. Enjoying myself.

—He's finished, I said. —Out of here.

Then I hit him again, to prove that I was right.

—There, I said.

I went to the sink and filled the pan with cold water. Charlo wasn't going anywhere for a while. I remember the weight of the water going into the pan. I remember deliberately turning on the cold tap because I wanted to save the hot. Nicola grabbed the salt cellar off the table. It's one of those heavy ones made from marble. We still have it but the pepper disappeared years ago. She looked down at Charlo. She wanted to hit him — he was starting to get up. I was turning off the tap, spilling some of the water because the pan was too heavy for me. She looked like a young one surrounded by snakes and tarantulas. She couldn't move.

Then John Paul came in. (I hate thinking about John Paul. I'm not ready yet.) He came into the kitchen.

—What's going on? he said.

His face, the puzzled look he'd had since he was a baby. He was in his pyjamas — stripey bottoms and an Italia 90 t-shirt. He was holding onto the bottoms.

—Get back up to bed, love.

I tried to sound normal. With his da in a heap on the floor.

—What happened my da?

—Get up to bed, I said.

—Me da, but.

—Get up!

I roared at him. It kills me now, the number of times I roared at him, screamed at him. And hit him. Jesus, I even kicked him. I roared at him more often than I kissed him. God, he was so small.

He wouldn't go.

Charlo was on his knees now, coughing like he was going to get sick.

—What did yis do to him? said John Paul.

What did *yis* do to him. Not just me. Me and Nicola. The women.

I didn't roar again, I'm fairly sure of that.

—There's nothing wrong with him, I said. —Now go on. Please. You can come down in a minute.

—But he's —

—I had to teach him a lesson, I said. —Go on up. He's alright.

I watched him turning and going. He was angry, and humiliated. He glared at Nicola. (I never spoke to him about it again.) Something moved. I jumped. It was Charlo shaking his head.

—Fuckin' hell, he said.

He sounded like he'd rehearsed the words. He sprinkled his blood around him. It was the first time I'd noticed it. He was bleeding quite badly. It was soaked into his shirt and on his trousers. I poured the water over him, leaned over him so his hands couldn't grab my legs. His hair hung over his face and for a second I thought he looked funny and lovely. It froze him. He hadn't a clue where he was.

—Get out of here, I said.

I was ready to hit him again. I looked at Nicola.

—Open the front door, love, I said.

His blood was drip-dripping again after all the water. He lifted one knee and tried to stand up.

—What are you — ?

I hit him again, hard, as hard I as could let myself. There was no way I was going to give him the chance to talk to me, to even think. My mind was made up and he wasn't going to change it. I wasn't going to let him.

—Get out; go on. And you're not coming back.

He started to get up again. I had to let him. I couldn't get him out if I didn't. The groans and grunts out of him, I'd never heard him like that before. (He broke his leg in a football match and I was watching it on the sideline — before we got married; I went to all his matches — and the noise of him, he was in absolute agony. I ran on to the pitch. I'd have gone for the fella who'd tackled him and scratched his eyes out if I'd known which one it was. They were all the same size and covered in muck.

—Fuckin' bastards!

—Take it easy, said someone. —It was a fair challenge.) The noise he was making now, it reminded me of the noise a toddler makes when she's trying to stand up after falling down, big gulps and effort and strain and concentration. I couldn't let him stand up straight. I gave him a push the second his legs began to unbend and he fell into the hall — it was hardly any distance. I clattered him on the back to keep him down. He crouched and moved down the hall. I wouldn't, I couldn't let him settle. He spoke.

—Stop, will yeh.

I kept up with him, got between him and the stairs and shoved him to the door. Nicola left it wide open and jumped onto the stairs. He was coming straight at her, like a big old cow coming out of a tunnel. She jumped up onto the stairs.

—Paula —

—Fuck off; get out — !

I hit him and shoved, kept him stunned. He missed the door. He bashed up against the wall, knocked and smashed the holy water font. Part of it still hung on its nail. There hadn't been water in it in years. A broken cobweb swung above it. I slapped him towards the door, just a bit more.

Leanne and Jack were on the stairs.

—Leave him alone!

It was John Paul.

Charlo shut the door. I don't know how; I don't think he meant to. He went too far, past the open door, hit the wall, turned and brought the door with him; he was hanging onto it. Nicola screamed. John Paul pushed her down a step, nearer Charlo. She backed up past him — she'd have killed him to get away from Charlo. She shoved and panicked her way past him, up to Jack and Leanne. God love her, maybe she thought that Jack would save her. His little sleepy face looking down, he hadn't a breeze what was happening. Charlo fell against the door. I grabbed his hair — he liked it long, thank God — and I pulled him away from the door, yanked some of it out of his head. I didn't care. I didn't think about caring. I didn't think at all. Terror made me brave. I reefed him up, back towards the kitchen.

—Open the door! I yelled at John Paul.

—Leave him alone!

—Open the fuckin' door!!

He did it. I don't know why. Maybe in the back of his head he knew what was best. Maybe I looked like a madder bitch than his father.

221

I kicked Charlo.

I kicked him out the door. He slid out. He turned like a seal in the water and slid out. I wasn't finished yet. I went after him. I had to push poor John Paul out of my way. Jack had started crying now. Nicola picked him up.

I hounded him to the gate. I never let him straighten up or get his head together. I didn't hit him again. I didn't have to. I was frightening him. I escorted him off the premises. Out the gate he went. He got away from me, down the path, away from us. Drenched and bloody and stooped over like a travelling rat.

Then I began to think.

Oh Jesus.

I got back to the door. I ran the last yards. It was only starting. What was going to happen now? I was an eejit for thinking that I could get rid of him that easily, that I could ever get rid of him. He was going to kill me, kill us all. It was only fuckin' starting.

I looked. He was coming back. He was walking back.

—Go away!

I stood my ground. I wanted to dash inside.

—Go away!

He stood there. At the gate. The blood was still running out of his head, down into one of his eyes. The door behind me slammed. I turned enough to see through the glass. It was Nicola. She stayed there, ready to open the door when I shouted. I hoped.

He still stood there, just stood. He didn't come in. He just stood there. He swayed. Like the scarecrow from The Wizard of Oz. His head was down. He stared at me through his hair. His shirt was soaking. His arms were at his sides, held out from his sides like he was going to draw his guns and shoot me. But he didn't have any guns.

Not back then.

—Go away, will yeh! Go away!

And he did. I couldn't believe it. He did what I'd told him to. He walked away. His head still down. He said nothing at all.

Suddenly, I was very scared. I knocked on the door now, really hammered it. I was terrified.

—Let me in.

He was going to come after me.

—Let me in!

He knew he was scaring me, was already making the most of what had happened. Already recovering and taking over.

—Nicola; hurry up! Come on.

Putting me back in my box. He was going to demolish me.

She opened the door.

What had I done, what had I done?

—Hurry up!

I pushed the door into her and got into the hall. I didn't look back. There wasn't time.

—Jesus —

Nicola shut the door and locked it. She looked calm now. She looked at me.

—Jesus —

I was shaking. I sat on the bottom step. I'd look at the kids in a minute. I'd be ready then. I got up and looked through the pebbly glass. No Charlo. I pressed my face and saw as much as I could see. No. He wasn't there. Nothing on the path. Nothing at the gate. Nothing in the hedge.

—He's gone.

I looked at Nicola. She wanted to believe me.

—For now, I said.

That relaxed her; it was realistic.

—I think I might have skulled him, I said. —Really skulled him. He was looking very queer.

I laughed first. She followed me. I've always laughed in the wrong places.

—Hasta la vista, baby, I said.

Then I saw John Paul. I wanted to hug him, he looked so miserable and angry. He was looking at a pair of bitches laughing.

—What did he do? said John Paul.

I put my arms out for him. They were aching. I wanted to hug his sadness into me.

—Come here to me, I said.

I was sure he would. I needed him to. But he wouldn't let me touch him. He slapped one of my hands away.

—Lay off, will yeh.

God.

—What did he do?

I should never have tried to grab him. He felt that I was insulting him, treating him like a baby. It was just that my head wasn't right; I wanted to hug all my children, make sure that I still had them. Especially John Paul.

—I'll tell you sometime, I told him.

It was too late.

—You'll understand.

He turned — his face, Jesus, it was breaking up — and he ran back up the stairs. He barged through the other kids. He went out of his way to hurt them. He slammed his door. I left him there for the day.

He never understood. I never spoke to him about it.

I looked at Nicola and reminded myself of what was

going on. She shrugged. I shrugged back. It was strange; I was happy and worried. She let me hug her. And Leanne and Jack.

—What now? said Nicola.

—God knows, I said. —But one thing's for certain. He's not coming back in here again.

Her face said it: she'd heard it before.

—He's not, I said. —I'll bet you a tenner.

—Okay, said Nicola.

It was a great feeling for a while. I'd done something good.

30

There was the yellow accident tape warning people not to go near. One of the Guards stepped over the tape and walked away from the camera. The camera homed in on the car. Charlo was beside it, with the blanket over him. He was face down; his foot was hanging from the open door.

He couldn't drive. That was why he'd got out of the car again. The poor eejit, he never got round to it. The kidnapper who couldn't drive. He didn't have a licence, he'd never had a car — he'd never learned how to drive. He saw the guards coming over the wall, he shot Missis Fleming and ran to get away in a car he couldn't drive. It looked like he'd tripped getting out of the car. It was neatly parked, a green Ford Escort. He'd fallen out onto the path. The houses looked nice. He was far from home.

31

—What now? said Nicola.

—God knows, I said. —But one thing's for certain. He's not coming back in here again.

She'd heard it before.

—He's not, I said. —I'll bet you a tenner.

—Okay, said Nicola.

It was a great feeling. I'd done something good.

Roddy Doyle

THE COMMITMENTS

'Brilliant...it pushes Irish English to wonderful imaginative extremes'
Tom Paulin

'A contender for the funniest debut of the year...young, feisty, funky, rude, unpretentious and great fun'
Time Out

'An absurd comedy of the commonplace...a charming, truthful and immensely funny story which leaves you gasping for more'
Sunday Times

'An Irish version of The Blues Brothers...authentic and brilliantly funny' *Literary Review*

VINTAGE

BY RODDY DOYLE
ALSO AVAILABLE IN VINTAGE